THE
PUNCH
BOOK
OF
SHORT
STORIES

THE
PUNCH
BOOK
OF
SHORT
STORIES

Selected by *Alan Coren*

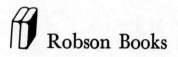

Robson Books

FIRST PUBLISHED IN GREAT BRITAIN IN 1979
IN ASSOCIATION WITH PUNCH PUBLICATIONS
BY ROBSON BOOKS LTD., 28 POLAND STREET,
LONDON W1V 3DB. THIS COLLECTION COPY-
RIGHT© 1979 ROBSON BOOKS

British Library Cataloguing in Publication Data
The 'Punch' book of short stories.
   1. Short stories, English
823'.9'1FS   PR1309.S5

   ISBN 0–86051–067–0

Set in 11-12 Garamond by Ronset Ltd., Darwen Lancs and
printed in Great Britain by Billing & Sons Ltd., Guildford,
London and Worcester.

CONTENTS

PREFACE

The short story is a threatened species. As its natural habitat, the literary magazine, shrinks, changes, decays, vanishes, there is almost nowhere for it to turn for nourishment and hope. Here and there, those sad and worthy enterprises, the Little Magazines, bob against the commercial tide for a season or two like ramshackle rafts, and you will generally find a couple of short stories lashed to their unstable masts; but they go under.

And writers, with livings to make and reputations to build, turn inevitably elsewhere, towards more marketable forms. Tragic, this; for the short story is a distinct and invaluable genre, not (as some would have it) a literary curio: there are things which had to be said by Poe and Chekhov and Maupassant and Kipling, by Henry James and Katherine Mansfield and Max Beerbohm, by Saki and Maugham and Joyce, by Hemingway and Graham Greene and Salinger and Borges, that could be said only over the furlong. Often, short fiction was the best of these writers, and many others; the novels ran out of wind, or filled with it.

But while I am concerned for the loss of those subtleties, those deftnesses, those concentrations and nuances that are special to the short story, it was the qualities rather than the pity for their imminent doom that persuaded me, when I took over the editorship of Punch, to run a weekly story in its pages. Because conservation for its own romantic sake is as rotten a way to run a paper as it is to run a railroad: it is purposeless to keep a branchline open if its platforms remain deserted. In the event, the short story proved to be our most popular innovation: readers hailed it, writers stacked our in-trays, a new and special quality came into the magazine.

This book is a selection of our 1978 stories. Next year, we shall publish a selection of our 1979 ones. And the year after that . . .

Salmon are back in the Thames, too. A good fish, the salmon.

ALAN COREN

PAUL THEROUX

The English Adventure

'You have read already *The Times*?'

'I just did so.'

'For my lateness I am deeply sorry, but there was the parking. So much of traffic in this town now. I think it is the Germans and their campings. It is fantastic.'

'I hate the campings. And the Germans are a shame. You see? There are some at that table. Listen to them. Such a language.'

'I much prefer the English.'

'Indeed. Quite so.'

'Why are you drinking *genever* at this hour?'

'For *The Times*. I had the tea and finished it. But there was still more of *The Times*. I could not have more tea, so I took some *genever*. And so I finished *The Times*, but I still have the *genever*.'

'Henriet! You will be drunk for Janwillem!'

'It is easier to speak English if one is drunk, and tonight is Janwillem's church.'

'A lousy night for Janwillem.'

'He likes the church, Marianne. Last week he has missed the church and he has been so ashamed.'

'I mean that. Happy as a louse on a dirty head. We say "a lousy time" for a happy time.'

'We say a jolly time.'

'A jolly time. Thank you. Did you learn this in *The Times*?'

'I learned this in England.'

'Have you had a jolly time in England?'

'A lousy time.'

'Henriet! You are drunk already. So I will have the tea. Last week, I had the tea, but no English. I said to the boy, "One pot of tea and two cakes, if you please." But he did not reply in English. It was so insulting to me. I think he did it to be wicked. When he brought the tea I said, "Please," but he only smiled at me. I was so deeply sorry you were not here. You would have said more.'

'The young boy?'

'The old boy.'

'I would have said more.'

'I have been thinking last week of you in England. Proper tea, proper English. I know you already for ten years, but since we are starting this English I know better. "Lucky Henriet," I have been thinking last week, "in London with the plays and the shows, and speaking English to all the people. And I have nothing but this news and this wicked boy." You buy that shoot in London?'

'I have bought this suit in London.'

'Please. And the weather, it was nice?'

'London weather. London rain.'

'It is fantastic. And the hotel, it was good?'

'We will not speak of the hotel.'

'Janwillem, he enjoyed?'

'Janwillem is Janwillem. Here he is Janwillem, and in another place we go—how much money, tickets, taxis, rain, different people—he is still Janwillem. In London, at the hotel, we are in the room and I am sitting in the chair. I look out the window— a small square, with grass, very nice, and some flowers, very nice, and the wet street, so different. I turn again and I am happy until I see Janwillem is still Janwillem.'

'You are not going to speak of the hotel, you say!'

'I was mentioning my husband.'

'He is a good man.'

'Quite so, a good man. I love him. But even if he had a few
faults I would love him. I would love him more and wish him to
understand. The faults make the love stronger. I want him to be a
bit faulty, so I can show him my love. But he is a good man. It
is so hard to love a good man.'

'Your English is fantastic. It is London. Last week I am here
with this tea and this old boy. I am learning nothing. You are
learning more English. It is London.'

'It is this *genever*. And my sadness.'

'We will then speak of the news. You have read already?'

'And the hotel and Janwillem. So many times I ask of him to
understand this thing. "No," he says. "Do not speak of it." And
he goes to his church. Even in London—the church, he is missing
the church. And the children and the house. He is a good father,
such a good one. But at the church, I have seen him three weeks
ago, a festival, he is dancing with the other ladies, hugging them.
He is so happy. Kissing them and holding hands. What is wrong
with that? A man can do such things and it means nothing, but a
woman cannot. No hugging—this is the fault. For a man it
means nothing. He is going home in the car laughing, so happy
while I am so very sad.'

'I have read the front page, Henriet. And some letters. Have
you seen "appalling lack of taste"? We can discuss.'

'I have seen "appalling lack of taste" and I have seen the programme on television to which it is referring.'

'Fantastic.'

'But I cannot discuss. I will have another *genever*. See? He
knows I want it and I have not been asked. Such a pleasant boy.'

'He is the boy who insulted me.'

'It is only natural, Marianne. You speak in English. He is
wishing to be friendly.'

'I do not wish to be friendly.'

'He is not the old boy. He is the young.'

'I am drinking tea. He is the old.'

'Perhaps he would enjoy an adventure. It means nothing to

them.'

'We shall speak of the news instead.'

'It is the thing Janwillem does not understand at all and he will never understand. "Do not speak of it!" But if he has an adventure I can understand. I can love him more. But he has no adventure. I have told you about Martin?'

'The librarian. He gives you books.'

'He gives me pinches.'

'We shall talk of the books.'

'And he tells me how easy it is. It means nothing to him. He wants me to spend the night with him. I tell him impossible. An afternoon, he says. After the lunch period he puts the library in the hands of his assistant and we leave. To my house. Four hours or five. Before Janwillem comes home, before Theo breaks from school. How does he know it is so easy? But he knows too much about this. How does he know? I ask him. He has three girl-friends, or two—anyway, more than one. He boasts about them, and of course I cannot have an adventure with Martin. He would boast of me.'

'Maybe he would boast of you.'

'Or talk about me. Men talk.'

'Janwillem would be so sad.'

'Janwillem would kill me. He could not stand it. I wonder if I can stand it? One day I am home with my throat—one afternoon. I am walking around the house. Strolling around the house. Not in our bedroom. Janwillem's clothes are there. He is so neat. In Theo's room. Yes, I think, that is where we would have our adventure. I go into Theo's room. Stamp collection, maps, Action-Man.'

'Fantastic.'

'I cannot have an adventure in my son's room with Martin. Action-Man. It would make me sad.'

'I am glad I am older than you, even if my English is not good. But we will go to Croydon in April.'

'In London it is wonderful even in the rain. The people are

different, and so polite. If you speak to them they speak. If you
don't speak to them they speak. If you don't speak they are still
polite.'

'*The Times*—it is very cheap in Croydon. Is it cheap in London?'

'I never read the newspaper, not once. Janwillem read it. I saw
him reading it and I did not want to. I can read it here, but not
there. There, I can read novels, only novels. In the hotel room,
having some gin, with the rain outside, and Janwillem in his
offices. No Theo, no Action-Man. There I am different, too. No
headaches. I was so worried about Martin I began the migraines.
Always on my day off—the migraines. And we did nothing! He
only boasted and pinched, and I said, "Yes, it is a good idea, an
adventure, but not here".'

'This talk is a bit silly and it is shaming me. Shall we discuss the
news? I still have some tea left. Or books? I have seen that there
is a new novel by Mister Dursday.'

'Tom Thursday. Extremely violent. He shows an appalling lack
of taste. I wish to speak of thumsing else.'

'I have read all his books. Tom's.'

'Do you remember that young American fellow—Jewish
fellow—he spoke of the American novel to the Society?'

'He was fantastic.'

'He asked me to meet him. That young fellow. How could I
meet him? I have my family to think of, I have Janwillem. I
cannot simply go off because this young Jewish fellow wishes to
have an adventure. He writes me letters: "Come! Come!" I
think he is like Martin.'

'Martin is not Jewish. You never said so.'

'Martin and his boasting and his girl-friends.'

'Do not think of him, Henriet. He will give you migraines.'

'Martin is gone, but I shall have the migraines. I have to
scream sometimes because of the migraines. Do you ever scream,
Marianne?'

'I like this. This is better. Yes, one day I was making some
soup. Some carrot, some potato and chicken broth. I am looking

for the, yes, the barley. The soup was in an enormous pot. The soup was boiling furiously. It was a very hot day. And then I reached for the barley. The barley was on a high shelf. I reached for it. I hit with my elbow the pot of soup and it splashed upon my arm. And then I screamed.'

'I scream at Janwillem because he is so good. He mentions the church and I scream. I scream when I think of Martin, and Martin is bad.'

'As you say, Martin is wicked.'

'Martin is not wicked, but I cannot trust him. Always his girl-friends. I would prefer to have an adventure with another man.'

'I am too old for adventures, Henriet. And this is not the place.'

'Those Germans—they drive twenty kilometres and have their adventures here. Look at them. You're not looking.'

'I have seen Germans.'

'The English people hate them as much as we do. But some do not even remember.'

'How can they remember the Germans? If once you see them you remember!'

'The young ones. They do not remember.'

'Even the young ones remember!'

'In England.'

'The young ones in England? I do not know the young ones in England. This tea is cold. How do you know?'

'I have asked.'

'What do they say?'

'They do not know. They do not care now. It is old history.'

'Where do you meet these young ones?'

'I meet them in England. In London.'

'In the hotel.'

'Yes, in there.'

'I have not met them in Croydon.'

'Do you know young ones in Croydon?'

'Henriet, everyone I meet is younger than me. So I do not notice.'

'I notice. The young ones remind me.'

'That they are young?'

'That I am old.'

'But you are not old. What? Forty-five? Very slim and smart. Nice shoot.'

'Forty-three.'

'It's not old.'

'If you are twenty, forty-three is old.'

'This is good English conversation. Question-answer. Those Germans must think we are two English ladies, having our tea.'

'I am not having tea.'

'You know what I am saying.'

'I did not have tea in London. In London, Janwillem has tea, he reads *The Times*, he takes his umbrella. People think he is a schoolmaster. In London, I sit by the window and read my novel and watch the rain fall. And I wait—what for? For the young to knock on my door and say, "Madam, your adventure".'

'You are being silly.'

'In a uniform. A dark jacket and a small black tie and a tray. My adventure is on the tray. "Just one moment," I say. And I get up from my chair and pull the curtains so that he won't notice my age. I am very nervous, but he is more nervous, so it does not matter. I go very close to him. If you go close and he does not draw away, you know he is saying yes.'

'Henriet, you have had too much to drink. Please, the news.'

'I am telling you the news.'

'This is not a discussion. We must discuss.'

'There is nothing to discuss. I need my adventure. I have gone to London with Janwillem for my English, but what is English if you cannot use it except to say, "Please close the door," and "Where is the post office?" and "How much?" Or if you only speak it once a week at a hotel-restaurant in a terrible town as this one is.'

'I enjoy it. It is good enough for me. I am happy.'

'I am not happy. English is not enough, Marianne. Books are

very enjoyable, and lectures. But always there is Martin in the library, and that American fellow at the lectures. I ask myself: "Am I here because of English, or do I want an adventure?"

'What is the answer?'

'There is no answer. But English is not enough, I know that. If that could be so I could sit in the chair in the hotel and talk with the boy and be happy.'

'There was a boy?'

'I have told you of the boy. With the tray and the tie. Twenty. English. Thin face. Very nervous.'

'You talked with him in English?'

'Very little.'

'You are smiling. No more English.'

'I can only tell you in English.'

'You have said you talked very little.'

'He took his clothes off, I took my clothes off. We were naked. After that, there is very little to say. "We were naked." It is so easy to say, "We were naked," if you say it in another language. It would be harder to tell Janwillem—I couldn't say it to him in English. But he would not understand, would he? No, he would shout at me. "Do not speak of it!" and then he would go to his church and hug and kiss those women. And formerly, I had the migraine and I have thought all those years of shooicide. Instead, I have the lessons—we have them here. But in London I know why I have the lessons. It is clear to me there. The boy. We say very little because we both can speak. So we don't need to speak. It is a small thing. As for Janwillem, it means nothing. Now we are here and it is gone, but it is not gone. There is only the English.'

'A good lesson today, Henriet.'

'Yes, Marianne.'

'Some new words. A jolly time.'

'We will say no more about my adventure.'

'Next week we will read *The Times*.'

'I will drink tea.'

'You are fantastic.'
'Yost so. Dat is da most faluable ting.'

ALEXANDER FRATER

The Emir

Mr Safrani was appointed Director General three weeks after the television station was formally opened by the emir. He replaced Mr Mohamed who died of a stroke during the public uproar that followed the telling, by an aspiring comedian—now assembling Volkswagens in Germany—of a profane joke on the *Tuesday Talent Show*. Mr Safrani, a tall, bony, watchful man who kept his own counsel, had been editor of a respected daily newspaper where he established a reputation for firmness and sobriety which, when he moved from his comfortable, shoddy downtown office up to the lofty chrome and leather suite at the top of the television station, he fully intended to preserve. His first act was the sending of stern letters to all the comedians on the station's books, telling them to clean up their material.

Privately, he didn't care much for television. He had watched it abroad, of course, and had witnessed the birth pangs of his own outfit under the troubled aegis of Mr Mohamed, but everything he had seen simply emphasised his preference for the strength and suppleness of the written word. Still, he was not without ambition and though, initially, he felt rather ill-at-ease with his staff, a querulous, competitive lot who wore fancy clothes and cursed like gypsies, he speedily established his authority and, within a few days, had made it clear who was master of this curious new household.

It was during this period that the emir paid his first visit. Mr

Safrani was at his desk, drafting a letter relating to the purchase of an hour's satellite time each day—as an old reporter, one of his most urgent self-appointed tasks was the beefing up of the news bulletins—when Miss Aswan, his secretary, buzzed him excitedly to say that the royal helicopter was approaching. Mr Safrani slipped on his jacket and stepped out onto the roof. The machine, an Alouette painted a brilliant kingfisher blue, had just beaten up a visiting cruise liner down in the harbour and was climbing fast towards Mr Safrani. He had flown with the emir on a number of occasions and was familiar with his foibles at the controls. Now he came over the roof in a howling, skidding turn, the rotor thundering like gunfire, and braked hard. The Alouette spun 180 degrees on her axis, tilted sharply forward then descended, gently as thistledown, for a tidy landing.

The emir wore battle fatigues and was covered with dust. He had been on manoeuvres with the army in the arid plains south of the tablelands, and looked as though he had not left his tank turret for a week. His companion, a young artillery officer, remained in the machine, motionless and ashen-faced beneath his own coating of dust.

'Well, well, my friend, and how goes it?' said the emir, shaking hands with Mr Safrani. He jerked his head at the officer in the Alouette. 'My new ADC,' he said. 'Sandhurst-trained and *very* good, but still unblooded when it comes to hard flying. Have a drink sent out to him, then take me to your office and give me one too. My throat feels like a leper's armpit.'

Mr Safrani dispatched Miss Aswan, beaming anxiously, for chilled orange juice, and conducted the emir to an armchair in the coolest corner of the suite. 'The manoeuvres were successful, I hope,' he said.

'Moderately,' said the emir, peering abstractedly at the silent, flickering monitor opposite Mr Safrani's desk. 'The Canberras will have to go, though. Too old, too slow: during the ground attack exercises they could barely catch my Supply Officer's mules. I would give my right arm for a couple of squadrons of

Mirages.' He gestured at the monitor. 'What's this?' he said.

'*Kiddies' Corner*, sir. A children's programme.'

The emir nodded and Mr Safrani, noting his interest, paid attention. A large green frog was engaged in conversation with a startlingly good-looking girl—eyes the colour of ferns, tawny hair cropped short with small, crisp curls about the neck, an air of repose and inner stillness that seemed to imply unfathomable spiritual depths. Casting an eye down the day's Running Order he noted that her name was L. Nahayyan and, when the emir's question came, as he knew it would, he was able to identify her at once. 'Turn up the sound, old man,' said the emir.

Mr Safrani adjusted the switch. '. . . trout sleeping under my water lily,' said the frog, starting to move about unsteadily, 'and waking me up with his snoring. It's really too bad!' He gave a clumsy, ill-timed leap, tripped and nearly fell into the pond. Mr Safrani frowned and picked up his red telephone. 'Is that frog drunk?' he said.

'No, Mr Safrani,' said the deputy producer. 'It's his war wound. The actor lost a kneecap fighting for the Loyalists in the 1964 Rebellion. He must jump to indicate his anger with the trout for sneaking under his leaf.'

Mr Safrani sighed and hung up, remembering wistfully that this was the hour when he and his leader-writers met to discuss, over coffee, the day's burning issues and weighty matters. The emir said, 'I think I shall go down and take part in this programme.'

'Sir?'

'I wish to speak to the children of my country.'

Mr Safrani called the startled director, who said that the emir could be accommodated when the show concluded, in three minutes' time. They descended to the studio in Mr Safrani's private lift and, when the frog and the trout had concluded a stilted little dance, applauded by the girl, the emir took their place by the pond. A spotlight flicked on and caught him, fair and square, in mid-beam. He stood there, a small, slim man, full of gravity, authority and seriousness of purpose, with white dust on his clothes, on his face, in his hair, steadily meeting the light's hot, golden eye. He spoke without introduction or preamble, a little homily urging the nation's children to be obedient, to study hard, to eat their meals, go to bed early and prepare for useful, rich and fruitful lives in the years ahead. The frog stood to attention throughout, while the trout nodded to emphasise the emir's points and Miss Nahayyan gazed at him with her lips parted.

Afterwards, before leaving the studio, he spoke to her quietly for several minutes, and Mr Safrani noted that her cheeks were flushed and her movements rather agitated. In the lift, ascending to the penthouse suite, the emir said, 'She is an actress.'

'Quite so.'

'I am taking her home. She lives in an apartment on Suwaidi Street. I can land in the football stadium.'

Miss Nahayyan, wearing a short lime-green dress, came to the suite shortly afterwards, escorted by the Head of Children's Programmes. The emir led her to the Alouette. 'I have a passenger,' he said to the ADC, 'with whom I wish to talk privately. You will have to make your own way.'

'But I've got no money,' said the ADC, clearly affronted.

'Borrow some from Mr Safrani.'

He touched a forefinger to his crimson helmet then lifted off and flew west, straight and level, while Mr Safrani led the sulking ADC to Miss Aswan's petty cash box and gave him his taxi fare back to the palace.

Mr Safrani had vague premonitions of trouble, and these were confirmed two days later when, late in the evening of another scorching day, the Alouette returned. The emir, fresh and dapper in a lightweight grey suit, walked in and lit a cigarette. Then, speaking slowly, emphasising his words with small, neat gestures of the hands, he said that Miss Nahayyan's great abilities must be celebrated as soon as possible. A major drama production was to be mounted. She was to star. The country's best actors were to appear in the supporting roles. 'She yearns,' he said, 'to play

Lady Macbeth.'

Mr Safrani listened with a sinking heart. He had made en-
quiries about the girl, and had been advised, most emphatically,
that she possessed no talent whatsoever. The Head of Drama
himself had said that she could manage only two expressions: the
expression of a woman being stung by a wasp, and the expression
of a woman not being stung by a wasp. Choosing his words with
extreme care, chiselling, balancing and considering them as
deliberately as though dictating an editorial, he attempted to put
matters into perspective.

The emir was unperturbed; perhaps he didn't believe him. 'Her
beauty will carry the day,' he said. 'Her goodness will shine
through. She has no need of those little tricks and mannerisms
that other actors employ. She will play it from the heart.' He
nodded at the monitor. 'What's that?'

'*Window on the World*, sir. The current affairs programme.
Tonight we are dealing with declining standards in our hospitals.
We have a panel of doctors defending charges of carelessness,
malpractice and so forth.'

'A timely issue,' said the emir, 'about which I should like to
speak. I will join them.'

He slipped onto the set during a three-minute videotape
sequence on conditions in the Outpatients' Department at the
City General and, back live, did not mince his words. He told the
panel of doctors to use clean instruments, administer the right
dosages, improvise when the proper equipment was lacking,
show initiative, be resourceful, remember their Hippocratic
Oaths and work for the common good. Then he asked them,
courteously, whether they wished to discuss any of the points he
had raised. Dazed, they shook their heads. He smiled at them,
embracing them all with that limpid gaze, then accompanied Mr
Safrani back to the roof. Aboard the Alouette, he switched on the
instrument lighting and sat there, bathed in its dim malarial
glow. 'At school, in Massachusetts, I once played Banquo's
Ghost,' he said, reflectively, then slammed the door. The motor

coughed, the blades began to swish and Mr Safrani retired to his office and summoned the Head of Drama—whose response to the emir's proposal was crisp and uncharitable.

'Not only does he go after women like a ferret,' he said, 'but he loves to woo them with the extravagant gesture. Rumour has it he had to be restrained from making some Danish air hostess Honorary Commodore of Bomber Command. But Nahayyan playing Lady Macbeth? The mind boggles.'

'So what do we do?' said Mr Safrani.

'Nothing. Play for time. Tell him Shakespeare is held in very low esteem here. Tell him we'd get lousy viewing figures. Exaggerate the production costs. Keep throwing up objections.'

HD had once run illicit antique scrolls into Beirut, most successfully, and Mr Safrani respected his judgement. He determined to tackle the emir about the matter of budget and costs on his next visit. That, however, began inauspiciously. He came howling out of a blue, cinnamon-scented dusk and banged the machine down with such force that Mr Safrani winced. The gleaming belly of the Alouette was pock-marked with buckshot fired from the muzzle-loaders of dissident tribesmen. 'Ignorant oafs,' snapped the emir, running his fingers along the blemished, dimpled metal. He strode inside, threw himself into an armchair and snapped his fingers at Miss Aswan for orange juice. 'Is this your new quiz programme?' he said after a while, peering at the monitor.

'*Pop the Question*? Yes, sir.'

'Let me listen.'

Mr Safrani turned up the sound as a girl with protruding teeth and large, quoit-like earrings, speaking in the slurred accents of the northern provinces, said that the kiwi was a four-footed horned beast indigenous to Peru. 'God preserve us,' muttered the emir. Then a rough-hewn old fellow, who looked like a patriarchal goatherd, was unable to identify the occupant of Lenin's Tomb. 'Is it the Tsar?' he said, uncertainly, after prompting, and the emir clicked his tongue sharply. A plump housewife, asked

the function and purpose of NATO, said it was an organisation
to further the aims of European agriculture, and when a middle-
aged bus driver with ill-fitting teeth stated confidently that the
composer Beethoven was a Greek, the emir, exasperated, jumped
to his feet. 'Such ignorance!' he shouted. 'Such stupidity! Take
me down to the studio, Safrani.'

He strode onto the set, glared at the contestants sitting at their
table, then turned abruptly and faced the cameras. 'I am shocked
by the standard of knowledge displayed here tonight,' he said.
'Unfortunately, it is not confined to this studio. A cloud of back-
wardness and ignorance darkens the entire land. We have no
natural assets. We have not been blessed with oil, with minerals,
with great resources. Our only asset is our people, and a hell of
an asset they are turning out to be, I must say.'

He paused, scowling. There were grease smudges on his olive
green flying suit and, in the bright lights, he looked haggard and
tense. 'Read books!' snapped the emir. 'Sharpen your minds! Use
your wits! Consult the newspapers and understand the world.
Discuss the day's important events with your friends. Know about
other countries, other peoples. Educate yourselves! Knowledge
leads to wisdom and wisdom leads to prosperity. Think on that,
all of you.'

He walked quickly away and entered Mr Safrani's lift. 'Speaking
of wisdom, Safrani,' he said, suddenly calm, 'I must admit to a
lack of it when I proposed that Macbeth idea. It no longer in-
terests me and the project, consequently, is cancelled.'

Mr Safrani stared at him. 'Cancelled?'

'The girl would not be suitable. She is too moody, too emotional, too unstable. I find her company enervating in the extreme.
Actually, I am very tired. In a couple of days I go, incognito, to
Bangkok. The purpose of my visit is private. I need to rest, to
recharge my batteries.' He boarded the Alouette and rose into
the heavens like a clamouring star while Mr Safrani, who knew
about the emir's affection for Bangkok and the little Thai girls
who crawled over him in that city's pleasure houses, called HD

with the news. HD said praise be, that's a weight off our minds, a sentiment with which Mr Safrani fervently concurred. In good spirits, that night, he took his wife and daughter to dinner and a movie but the following afternoon his feeling of well-being vanished abruptly when the Head of Children's Programmes phoned. 'Layla Nahayyan has just turned up, fearfully late, for *Kiddies' Corner*,' she said. 'She missed rehearsal and I think she's been drinking.'

HCP was a thin, highly-strung spinster given to bouts of hysteria which shook her like fevers, but Mr Safrani took this information seriously. 'Then keep her off the set,' he said.

'But she has a central role in today's episode,' said HCP, her voice rising sharply. 'She also sings a duet with the frog and then leads the dance of the bandicoots.'

'The what?'

'A species of rodent, Director General.'

'Find her an understudy,' said Mr Safrani, 'rewrite the scripts, anything. Talk to the actors. See if they've got some ideas.'

When the show began, Mr Safrani cancelled all his appointments and concentrated on the monitor. The actors, he noted, were ad-libbing to cover Miss Nahayyan's absence, and were doing so quite inventively; he had just scribbled a draft memo of congratulation to HCP when, without warning, Miss Nahayyan walked on camera. She wore neither costume nor make-up and stood there unsteadily, smiling vacuously at the frog who stopped midway through a limerick, blanched and, setting the seal on Mr Safrani's mounting anguish, audibly took the name of God in vain. 'Hullo, boys and girls,' said Miss Nahayyan, her voice thick. 'I've been drowning my sorrows.' She giggled. 'Oh, my dears, so much wine and all because the emir can't cut the mustard any more. He blames me, but it wasn't my fault, really, and I want him to know that I still love him and I . . .'

Somebody sprang in front of her, waving a clipboard, gesturing frantically, and then the screen went blank. Mr Safrani remained frozen at his desk, wondering whether the emir had already left for Bangkok. A few moments later, however, he heard the Alouette approaching, its engine drumming, across the harbour. 'Is it true?' said the emir, his voice shaking. 'Did that bitch inform the world that I was impotent?'

'She only told the under sevens, sir,' said Mr Safrani.

'I must address the nation,' said the emir, 'at once. I shall explain that there is absolutely no truth in her allegations. Or possibly I should admit to a slight temporary problem? That I have been much preoccupied with matters of state?' He frowned, biting a thumbnail. 'No, damn it, I shall admit to nothing. I shall say it is a tissue of lies and that I am in excellent health.'

Mr Safrani knew he was about to lose his job and sat silently, considering the view from his window. He could see oily water, bumboats, godowns, the shabby boulevards and unkempt buildings of the town and, behind, the low, worn hills of the interior, lambent as glass in the clear lemon light, Everything was familiar, well-ordered, benign. But if he allowed the emir to bluster publicly about his virility then, given the almost mystical importance the people attached to such matters, the emir would be in big trouble. Mr Safrani contemplated the precise nature of the trouble—a discredited monarch, a demoralised army, a derisive population—and decided he wanted no part of it. Far better to let the matter die down of its own accord, the unattributable ramblings of a deranged girl. He cleared his throat and, speaking slowly, strongly advised the emir against proceeding to the studio.

The emir accepted this with bad grace, and asked for Mr Safrani's resignation. Then he walked from the suite, climbed into the Alouette, primed his machine guns and climbed away, rocking wildly, to shoot up some rogue camels in the western desert.

JACK TREVOR STORY

Soldier, Soldier

Dear Mr Rainham,
I don't remember the dead lady who said she was my wife. She
may not have been lying but it's a well-known trick on members
of Her Majesty's forces serving abroad. I don't fall for it myself. A
lady has to produce more evidence than three kids and a dropped
womb. I am writing in the matter of my defence. They have got
the wrong man. That lying creep from social security who said
he come to me and told me where they was living has got a
brother fighting for the IRA. His real name is Mahonnihy. I have
sources outside that have ascertained this fact for me. You check
on this before you go briefing my barrister. I would not set fire
to anybody's family let alone my own. The coroner was out to
get me, the middle-class sod. Ex-officers don't like cockney
soldiers up on murder charges.

Another thing is the year I was supposed to have married that
dead lady was 1957. That's too bad because I was in Singapore
that year living with a Chinese girl called Chi Chin. Ask anybody.
You say you checked the army records, but as I said in court
our unit was secret and unofficial. You will have to get access to
War Office secret files. Our unit was known as the AR which
stood for Artists' Rifles and is now called the SAS or Special Air
Services. We were an unofficial presence in South East Asia. We
was waiting to be dropped into Borneo. British soldiers were
killing in Borneo, Arabia and Java long before we broke into the

headlines at Suez.

My Chinese natural law wife and two daughters, Ping and
Pong, two and a half years old the youngest, were burnt to death
by British napalm bombing in Borneo. It happened only five
weeks after we had moved into the Caricao hutment. You notice
the coroner glossed over that didn't he? British napalm, old chap?
It's not British. Afterwards I and other British servicemen were
caught by the Nationalists and had all our toes broken with gun
butts so we couldn't run away. They had no prison to contain us
in a jungle situation. The day we were flown back to Stansted in
twenty-five Hercules aircraft we were exposed naked to tourists,
weren't we, hosed down in the forecourt of a package holiday
hotel, deliced, cropped, the lot, with all the American Polaroids
snapping at our testicles.

You may find that this is not in the military archives, Mr
Rainham, old man. They say 1959 was a quiet year. They told us
we were fighting for the Queen. I sliced a brown head in half
with a spade like cutting a melon. I was young, Mr Rainham,
patriotic to a fault. My first long-trousered suit was a Teddy-boy's
suit and my second was khaki. If there wasn't any killing to be
done for our government we used to get lent to the sheiks for
money—or women, or oil or goods, I doubt whether anybody
kept any records. We had an alcoholic padre, Eric, who was
writing a book, but he died in mysterious circumstances. I have
since tried to find his family, somewhere near Bicester, because
he was posting his manuscript home by instalments. Was there
ever another family burnt to death near Bicester, do you know?
Have you got fire insurance yourself? I have been trying to think
of possible witnesses.

You may like to talk to a Mr Reg Parker who is a brick worker
—last time I heard of him living at Toddington in Bedfordshire
and is also a S.A.S. reservist. He would be shot if he gave you any
details of our work abroad as I would be but he could confirm
about my dates and places and so on. He owes me a favour for
something that happened to a bookmaker in Hong Kong, tell

him. You will find he has a blue allegiance card like I showed you. We can be sent to any part of the world at a moment's notice, no option. I wish to hell they would send me somewhere now and get me out of this. They disown you if you get in trouble.

By the way, I have thought of another reason why my so-called daughter might have been raped before she was tied to the bedstead and burnt to death. I wouldn't do that just to avoid paying maintenance, would I? The reason I thought of is that a fireman did it. Martin Batesman was a fireman. We spent four nights inside a dead camel together as snipers. You wouldn't believe what happens sometimes at fires with everybody undressed and that. Look at it this way, Mr Rainham, Margery had been partially overcome by the smoke and she was lying across the bed with nothing on. She's got enormous knockers. Or so I was told. This fireman comes in. What? You think about it. I couldn't do a thing like that. I love children. If I hadn't gone in the army I would have been a teacher or social worker. I was always buying kids sweets in Cairo. Giving them rides.

You asked me to remember the name of my first probation officer in Clapham and I think it was Claydon. Mr Claydon. He was crippled for years. I used to push him round in his wheelchair. We all subscribed to getting him this chromium wheelchair. He used to run a club for us at the top of the Montagu Burton building with billiards and ping pong and soft drinks and the like. A good disco, plenty of tarts. That was when they wore those stiff little petticoats and you could see their arse when they twizzled. The trouble was Claydon used to preach at us. That's not the way to bring out the real qualities in kids. Anyway he fell down the stairs. Some families have rotten luck. Later on his wife was found drowned on Wimbledon common. You may remember. They thought it was probably suicide.

What offence had I committed to be on probation, you may well ask. Check the records and you will find I nicked some food out of Sainsburys in Clapham High Street and give it to an old age pensioner. Of course they couldn't find her when it come to the case. I hope to Christ you will be able to find Reg or Martin or somebody, Mr Rainham. They will give me a good character reference. If there is any slight hesitation, drop a hint that I might be out soon. Same if you find anybody hanging around at Christine's if you go to Milton Keynes again. Tell her I hope her arm is mending all right.

That was all over a packet of Cornflakes, incidentally. We only ever quarrel about little things. It was the way she tripped. Never lean your weight on furniture, that's one of the first things we were taught in unarmed combat—it might have been thrown before. She would keep coming in with these big packets. I've had this before with birds and I expect you have. They don't want marriage, they don't want babies, they want to stay free like you and live independent lives then suddenly one day they come home with a giant packet of Cornflakes or soapflakes. Chi Chin bought a whole sack of bean shoots just before she was burnt to death in Borneo. They all went up with her. Insecurity, that's what it is. My mum had an attic full of corned beef—well, three of my uncles are security men. All us Bates are in the law, army, security, police. That never come out in court.

Christine visited me yesterday. What did she have to say after forty-six lonely sleepless nights? 'Would you mind if I bought a huge box of broken biscuits? They're going cheap at Bludgeon's.' I've got a murder charge hanging over my head and she's thinking about big packets. The day the social security chap came and told her I'd got another wife and kids living off the nation Christine went out and got a carpet sweeper with Green Shield stamps. She believed all that rubbish in court. If the law says its true it's true. She's got a working-class mentality. She's terrified of uniforms. You could get her knickers off with a traffic warden's cap. I'm depending on you, Mr Rainham. All them other middle-class bastards are going to crucify me unless you do your stuff. And you'd better do it because if you don't I'm going to get out of this rat hole and I am going to follow you wherever you are and I'm going to stuff your bloody head up your bloody——I don't mean this in any nasty way. I just want you to realise that there is a certain degree of urgency.

Now, regarding the case for the prosecution when we come up at the assizes, I have been over all their so-called evidence with a Mr Priddle who is one of our warders who used to be a vet and also played golf. He considers that they have not got a case. It is Mr Priddle's considered opinion that unless they find the petrol can, or rather *a* petrol can, nobody can connect me with burning that family. That little fat swine suggested that's how I get rid of all my rubbish. I don't think you noticed it when he was giving evidence. You didn't jump up or anything. That little bastard is trying to suggest that I've been killing and burning prople all my life. Or knocking them downstairs like Mr Claydon, my poor crippled probation officer. And Mr Priddle says he's got no business to talk about my brother who got burnt to death stuck in a window. My own flesh and blood. We used to have rows, yes, but I never did any more than knock him out. Anyway he was a greedy bleeder. I think you ought to know the facts in case that prosecuting bugger comes up with anything different.

Now this is it, honest to God. My brother Hugo hated Aunt Sheba because she made him bath her when she had the rheumatics, the dirty bitch. One day he picked her feet up and drowned her, run out in a panic, knocked the oil heater over and tried to climb out the window with the broken sash. It come down on him, didn't it, when he was halfway out. Hugo never had no army training. I wasn't even there. I was screwing a bird in Basingstoke who I met when I was in tanks. Hugo's face never had a mark on it. His body inside the window was burnt to a cinder. When I hit somebody I mark them bad. All I got was the old woman's glass beads and the insurance worth sod all. I only took the policy out in case there wasn't enough to bury her. Or burn her.

And another thing. Mr Priddle says what happened in Borneo is not admissible evidence, Chi Chin and the kids being wogs and outside this jurisdiction. Anyway, I loved her. She had a lovely

body. I've got her picture stuck on this cell wall. I wanted to
bring her back home and get her a job with Mr Laser who does
this photomodelling stuff (that's another man you might contact
regarding the truth of this) but it meant leaving the kids with her
old Aunt Grisly—that's what I called her—and Chi Chin wouldn't
have it. Pity, as it turned out. You ought to have seen her corpse.
And the kids. Did you ever see napalm burn a body alive, Mr
Rainham? It sticks like tar and you can't put it out or get it off
they just frizzle while they're looking at you. It upsets me to think
about it. I can still smell them. You wouldn't pour it over your
worst enemy. Except that little fat swine.

   You go after him, Mr Rainham, now you have got the honest
to God sworn truth and testament on my oath to God and the
Queen and my mother's grave. She was burnt to death by the
incendiaries when I was ten. If she hadn't made me get evacuated
to Buckingham that might never have happened. Still, it's an ill
wind. Time I got out the army and was looking for a place to
live they was building the new city of Milton Keynes on my old
manor. There's a lot of my old oppos up there and a lot of villains
as well. And that's where the trouble came in really. These new
towns are like open prisons and stinking with fuzz. The old Bill's
friends and relations all working on the telephone exchanges.
That's how social security got on to me. I went down to Bletchley
and busted the place up didn't I—two miles of spaghetti down
the High Street. The telephone system was out of action for a
week, right up to Towcester. You ask Christine—her dad's a
postman.

   Wait a minute. I think I can smell something burning. You
just remember in case anything happens in this rat hole that I
have not been allowed matches or lighter ever since I was re-
manded in custody. It's all right now. That was Mr Priddle himself going past with his *meerschaum* special. It's an easy day today
they're all out playing cricket. Screws are not what they used to
be. Graduates some of them. Looking for a way into Special
Branch. You used to be able to trust your own kind. I have to be

careful with my writing and that. There's a few here don't want me to get into that bloody court.

By the way, keep Mr Priddle's name out of it he says else he can get struck off the prison service. He does something for me and I do something for him, don't I. I have shown him seven different ways of breaking out of this prison, no sweat. I have given him our SAS survival course. I have shown Mr P how to make indigestion powder out of wall scrapings and that. How to bite your way into a dead animal and live there amongst all the rotting entrails if necessary, waiting to get a pot-shot at somebody. How to get rid of dead bodies by chopping them into little lumps and getting them run over on the motor roads like hedgehogs. I can torture the truth out of the enemy with my thumb and forefinger only. Mr Priddle thinks you ought to mention this prowess in respect of the present British presence in Ireland and Brussels and so on. It would take five years to train somebody as good as me— and even then he would not have my natural instincts. For survival, that it.

I have been trained by my officers to bust out of this crappy prison any second I feel like it but I would rather have good old British justice. We SAS are the backbone of the country, the salt of the earth, says Mr Priddle. Where the flag is I will fight. I will tear any little fat swine to pieces with my bare teeth who lays a hand on our Queen. I seriously think you should mention this on my behalf, Mr Rainham. You seem too quiet.

Yours cordially
George K. Bates (Mr)
HM Forces (Res)
Remand prisoner 88zero zeroNJ 9B

Next time you are drinking with your friends at the golf club try to imagine how you would feel if you got home and your little daughter Zena had not come home from school. Mayfield, I believe it is. My sources outside tell me she arrives at Wimbledon South station at 4.30 every afternoon. But supposing she didn't?

Oh, daddy! Oh daddy! This is what my Christine is crying now
stuck up in Milton Keynes. And where am I? In this rat hole
with all my muscles. You better get me out, Mr Rainham. I can
still smell smoke . . . If they get me, this letter will still get to you
through the ventilation system and a dustman who shall be nameless. God Save The Queen.

RICHARD GORDON

Barnsfather's Syndrome

P_{aris} was a disappointment. Young Mr Edgar Barnsfather
FRCS had expected to find himself in the Champs-Elysées,
jammed between the Arc de Triomphe and the Eiffel Tower, with
the Folies Bergère opposite. The medical conference was in an
angular, concrete hotel like a hospital, a five-minute bus-ride
from the airport terminal. He had never been to France before.
He arrived in late afternoon, and queued for his conference
documents in the hotel foyer behind a fat, ruddy, gingery, rustic-
looking practitioner in tweeds.

'Awful bore, these conferences,' said the fat doctor genially.

'I wouldn't know,' Edgar replied meekly. 'I've never attended
one.'

'I'm only here for the beer. Exactly like everyone else. Dreadful
rackets, all scientific meetings. A most damning reflection on the
way we have to live. The doctors go along for a jolly, which they
can set against their income-tax. Some sinister drug company sub-
sidises it all for the publicity. As for the hotel, at this time of the
year they'd entertain a convention of cannibals to let their empty
bedrooms.'

Edgar could not help feeling shocked. 'I think myself privileged
to be delivering a paper.'

'Really? What about?'

'Barnsfather's syndrome. Pseudoperforation in young adults.'

'Ah! You're a surgeon?'

Edgar nodded. 'I'm a registrar at the Percival Pott.'

'An excellent London hospital.' The tweedy doctor smiled over half-moon glasses. 'And what *is* Barnsfather's syndrome?'

'I've a paper about it in the latest *BMJ*.' Edgar's voice was twisted painfully between pride and modesty. 'The first I've published, actually. I collected a series of young persons admitted with the signs and symptoms of acute perforated peptic ulcer. Abdominal pain, rigidity, vomiting, that sort of thing. But nothing physically wrong. All psychological. Stress, you know. Very interesting. Some were even operated upon. But perhaps this is not in your line?' he apologised.

'Not really.'

'And what do you do in the profession?'

'Oh, I just go on being President of the Royal College of Therapeutics.'

A pretty French girl in a thin white blouse stood behind a long table with piles of plastic-covered folders, each emblazoned in gold with the name of the drug company and the products it hoped the assembly would go home to prescribe. When Edgar introduced himself, she smiled delightedly and pinned to his lapel a card saying E BARNSFARTER.

'Have a nice time,' she said.

He stared at the lace edging her bra. He was full of unsurgical thoughts. It was his first night in two years of marriage away from his wife. The girl had given him such a lovely smile. 'Is there anything to do in the evenings?'

'There are excursions by autobus to the Opéra and Comédie française.'

'I mean of a more . . . er, intimate nature.'

'You like the *boxe*? There is a tournament just near the hotel.' She smiled delightedly at the next doctor. 'Have a nice time.'

Edgar bought a postcard of Napoleon's tomb, addressed it to his wife in Putney, but could find nowhere to post it. He slipped it in the pocket of his John Collier suit. He would take it home to put on the mantelpiece. It would save postage. He went up to his cuboid bedroom. It was getting dark. He gazed through the double-glazing at the wintry fields, the brightly-lit motorway, the ugly anonymous buildings which fringe all airports. Apart from seeing people drive on the right, he could have stayed at home.

He sat down with *Le Canard Enchaîné*, which he had extravagantly bought at Heathrow to get in the mood. He had been irritated at hardly understanding a word, having imagined that anyone with his intelligence and O-levels could read French. In the plane, he had thrown back his head and laughed loudly over the pages, just to show that he could, until the other passengers started staring at him oddly. So he had read through all the leaders in the *British Medical Journal*, his pale, domed forehead stamped with critical furrows.

He went carefully through the printed conference programme, received from the girl downstairs. He would be speaking the following afternoon to the psychosomatic section, between a surgeon from Chicago on the digestive processes of confused rats and a professor from Milan on phantom tape-worms in nuns.

He drew the *BMJ* from his briefcase, its handle secured at one end with a surgical suture. The learned pages fell open at the paper on Barnsfather's syndrome. He read it again all the way through, as though returning to the oft-folded sheets of a love-letter.

He sighed, staring through the window at the cars flicking along the motorway. This would be the first conference in a lifetime full of them. He might be a mere surgical registrar, but one day he would ease himself into a professorial chair. Everyone in the hospital told him that he was far more use in a lab than an operating theatre. He looked at his watch. It was dinner-time. He could savour the famed French cuisine.

Edgar crossed the foyer towards a notice saying:

INTERNATIONAL GASTROENTEROLOGISTS AND
CHOLECYSTOLOGISTS OFFICIAL DINNER

'Monsieur?' icily demanded a man in striped trousers at the door.

'Dinner,' Edgar explained. '*Dîner. Comprenez?*'

'Monsieur has an invitation? This is the dinner for the officials of the Congress. I assure monsieur that he will find an excellent dinner in the hotel restaurant.'

The restaurant was a long room hung with brown plastic curtains, so dim nobody could see the food or read the menu. He ordered *cervelle au beurre noir*, because he was fond of kidneys. He chose half a bottle of Beaujolais, because it was the only name he recognized. When the dish appeared, he realized that he had made an error in anatomy. The wine tasted peculiar, but he was too timid to complain. He ventured afterwards into the bar, but it was jammed with doctors drinking free brandy and noisier than students. He went to his room, undressed and read *Recent Advances in Surgery* until he fell asleep.

He woke. The curtains were drawn, the room pitch dark. He felt terrible.

He groaned, clasping his stomach. It was the brains, the wine. Some vile, explosive chemical reaction had occurred between the two. Brains always solidified in alcohol. That was how pathologists kept them, in pots.

He gasped. Colic tore at him with tiger's claws. He lay back on his pillow, breathing quickly. He was ill. He was also a doctor. He must decide what was wrong with him.

Intestinal obstruction? Appendicitis? Meckel's diverticulitis? Acute pancreatitis? Alarming diagnoses leapt through his mind, like questions fired at students over the bedside. The referred pain of coronary thrombosis, perhaps? Or of acute meningitis? Bellyache could be anything.

The tiger leapt again. He sensed sweat on his brow. He groped in the darkness. His watch said it was barely midnight. He fumbled for the telephone.

'*Allo?*' said a woman's voice.

'*Je suis malade.*'

'*Vous êtes Monsieur qui?*'

'*Malade*. Ill. Kaput. OK?'

'Monsieur wants room service?'

'No, I want a doctor.'

'*Oui*, monsieur. Which doctor?'

'Any doctor.'

'But monsieur! The hotel tonight is full of doctors.'

Edgar bit his thumb-nail. It was like having a riot at the police ball and dialling 999 for the squad cars. 'Has the hotel a doctor? One who comes when the guests are taken *malade*?'

'*Mais bien sûr*, monsieur. But he is in Paris.'

'Get him,' commanded Edgar, as another pang exploded in his stomach. An hour passed. The pains were worse. He was dying.

He picked up the telephone again.

'*Allo?*' said a man.

'*Je suis presque mort.*'

'*Ah! Monsieur désire quelque chose à boire?*'

Edgar put down the telephone. He rose, reaching for the red-spotted dressing-gown his wife had given him for Christmas. He staggered to the lift, descending with his forehead resting on the cool metal side. The foyer was empty. Edgar knew his materialisation was alarming, but desperate diseases needed desperate remedies.

'Why, there's the surgeon,' exclaimed the ruddy-faced President of the Royal College of Therapeutics. 'Sleepwalking, eh? Or astray on your way to some nice lady's bedroom? You surgical registrars, all guts and gonads. Or is there a fire?'

The official dinner was breaking up. From the door earlier barred to him drifted twenty or so doctors in dinner-jackets, all chattering noisily and slapping each other on the back.

'I'm ill,' said Edgar shortly.

'*Ill?*' The President was amazed. 'But you can't be ill here. We're all off duty. Enjoying ourselves at some crooked drug company's expense. Excellent dinner, Harry, don't you think?'

he enquired of a tall man swaying beside him. 'I'm so fond of
cailles à la gourmande. But of course, I should never dream of
paying for them.'

'The wine was fine, Sir Marmaduke,' said the tall doctor, an
American.

'I'm *so* glad you liked it. I chose it myself,' disclosed the President
smugly. 'I must confess a favouritism towards claret rather
than burgundy, and the Château Figeac '72 *is* very good. On the
other hand, the champagne they gave us—I say,' he added
irritably, as Edgar groaned loudly. 'Can't you do all that sort of
thing in your room?'

'I'm in agony.' Edgar doubled up. 'I've got an acute abdomen.'

'Really? Well, I suppose you should know. I'm only a physi-
cian. I never feel at home below the umbilicus.'

'Sir, Sir Marmaduke—' Edgar staggered towards him im-
ploringly. 'Can't you help me? I think I'm dying.'

'My dear fellow, of course, if *that's* the case,' said Sir Marmaduke more amiably, blowing into Edgar's strained face billows
of brandy. 'One has one's Hippocratic tradition, and all that, eh?
Human life must be preserved, however unworthy. Better have
a dekko at your belly. Just jump up there.' He indicated the table
previously supervised by the girl with the see-through blouse.
He pulled up Edgar's mauve pyjama-top and pulled down his
pyjama trousers. The other doctors crowded round. It was an
unexpected after-dinner entertainment.

'Where does it hurt?' asked Sir Marmaduke, staggering steeply
forward and pressing hard.

'Ouch!' screamed Edgar.

'Jolly interesting. You've got a retroperitoneal abscess.'

'Can anyone have a feel?' murmured Harry.

'My dear fellow, help yourself.'

'You're wrong, Sir Marmaduke,' Harry disagreed. 'It's a case
of haemoperitoneum.'

'Don't really think so, my dear old boy.' Sir Marmaduke had
his eyes closed. 'Patient would be more collapsed.'

'Ah! But they collapse and die suddenly. Like that.' Harry tried to snap his fingers, but missed.

'Excuse, please.' A Japanese doctor wriggled to the front, grinning. 'Please?' he asked, hand poised over Edgar's goose-pimples.

'Dear Saki-san, do plunge in. I'm sure we can all benefit from your oriental wisdom.'

'Please,' decided the Japanese. 'Clear case, hernia foramen of Winslow.'

'Now *that's* a jolly good diagnosis,' agreed Sir Marmaduke warmly. 'Any improvement on a herniated foramen of Winslow, gentlemen?' he invited, looking round.

'*Ja so*, we haf the jaundice?' asked another doctor, pulling down Edgar's eyelid.

'*Mon cher confrère*,' suggested another. 'This case reminds me of one I saw some years ago in Algeria. Ruptured amoebic cyst of the liver. Has your patient lived abroad?'

Edgar shook his head violently.

'Well, that is not necessary to get amoeba,' the French doctor consoled himself. 'My case was fatal, by the way. They nearly always are.'

'How about Legionnaires' pneumonia?' remarked another brightly. 'It's very popular just now.'

'Lassa fever can present like this,' came a voice from the back. 'Though of course I've never seen a case, nor even done a post-mortem on one. They whisk the bodies away so quickly in metal coffins.'

'Well, I must be toddling off to bed,' said Sir Marmaduke. 'Delightful evening. Delightful chaps. Don't forget the golf to-morrow, Harry. Anything to avoid the bloody papers.'

'What about me?' cried Edgar, sitting up.

Sir Marmaduke seemed to have forgotten him. 'I should get a glass of hot water from room service. Do you the world of good. Old remedies are best. If you're not better in the morning, toddle along to my suite and we'll have another prod.'

The doctors disappeared, yawning. Edgar crawled to the lift.
He fell into his bedroom. He dialled Putney.

There was a long wait. 'Who's that?' began his wife sus-
piciously.

'Edgar.'

She gasped. 'Did you miss your plane? God knows, you insisted on getting there early enough.'

'I'm in Paris—'

'What do you mean, phoning?' she demanded crossly. 'It's
dreadfully expensive. And at this hour, too. You scared me to
death. Or perhaps you imagined I was out for the night,' she
added cuttingly, 'and were just checking up on me?'

'I'm ill.'

'There're plenty of doctors to look after you.'

'They're all drunk.'

'What's the matter?' she asked with more concern.

'I've some sort of abdominal catastrophe. I'm coming home.
There's a plane at five a.m. I'll try and get on it.'

'But what about your paper?'

'It'll be printed in the Congress proceedings. I should have
liked to read it, but . . . what's the point, if I'm dead by tonight?'

'Oh, Edgar!' she cried. 'I'd no idea you were as bad as that.'

'I am. I must see a sober English doctor as soon as possible.'

'Oh, Edgar!' she said again, bursting into tears.

Groaning, gurgling, gagging, Edgar collected his luggage,
ordered a taxi, staggered into the airport, changed his ticket,
relaxed in his seat on the half-empty plane. He slept, exhausted.

He woke with the stewardess gently shaking him. 'Where am
I?' he cried in panic.

'We've just landed at Heathrow. Don't worry, sir,' she said
caringly. 'The captain had a radio message about you. You're in
good hands.'

She tenderly helped him to the aircraft door. He found himself
sitting on a fork-lift truck. Two uniformed men were waiting
below with a stretcher. They slid him into an ambulance, which

instantly raced across the tarmac with light flashing and horn blaring. A young man with glasses was leaning over him.

'I'm a doctor,' said Edgar.

'Are you? Well, so am I. Your wife alerted the airport. An acute abdomen, isn't it? I'd better take a look at it.'

He felt Edgar's tummy in silence. 'H'm.'

'What's the diagnosis?' Edgar asked anxiously.

'Without doubt, I'd say a clear case of Barnsfather's syndrome. There was a lot of guffle about it in this week's *BMJ*.'

JOAN BAKEWELL

Fault on the Line

Ring Ring. Ring Ring.

Jocelyn was baking bread when the phone rang. Not just any bread—pitta bread. Ever since their exquisite two weeks in a shepherd's hut on Hydra, Nick had been serving chilled ouzo before dinner. It kept their memories sweet, and impressed their friends and themselves with their own happiness. Now pitta bread—her contribution to keeping the idyll alive. How the sun had shone on them in Greece! Enough to make Tristram and Emma regret they'd opted for the Turkish coast where they'd got prickly heat and bickered all the time. Tristram and Emma were coming to dinner. Could this be a cancellation? It might be. Tristram was so busy, so important these days. She snatched the receiver with a doughy hand. It wasn't a cancellation. But it was Tristram.

'Hullo, Joss? Is that you—the gorgeous mistress, dare one say, of Lavenham Square?' Tristram embarrassed her. When she'd been his secretary he'd treated her with almost rude abruptness. Now she was Nick's wife, he'd switched to this ludicrous joviality. Neither made her feel easy. But she played along because he was now Nick's Head of Department. And she had the kind of heart that believed people were basically rather nice. She wasn't always right. In Tristram's case she met his exuberance with defensive banter.

'Tristram, how nice! Yes, it's me. Not actually gorgeous if you could see me now . . .'

'Absolutely refuse to believe it, Joss dear! In fact, I'm ringing
. . .'

'No truly . . . Up to the elbows in dough . . .'

'Well, only too delighted someone is, deary. The terrible truth
is, Joss . . .'

'You are coming, aren't you? We've had the kebabs marinading
for days and . . .'

'Yes, oh yes. Emma and I are longing for all that! She's driving
up from Dorset this afternoon—straight from pottery. No, I'm
actually ringing to see whether . . .'

'And trust Nick. He's found this special retsina—in a place
behind Camden Town. Just the same as . . .'

'Joss. Lovely, lovely. But later. At the moment I need to know
if Nick's there by any chance. I though he just could be . . .'

'No. Here? No, of course not. He's with you. That's where
he said he'd be.'

'Ah, is he? Yes. Good! You don't happen to know what he's
up to today, do you?'

'Yes, of course. He said he'd be editing all day. Definitely.
Tucked away in the cutting room. That film about how the
package boom is threatening the economy of the Third World.
He really thinks it's a good one. Been working all hours.'

'Of course, of course. Lucky sod. I don't know how I let him
get away with it, swanning round the Seychelles. Yes, I've tried
the cutting room. Perhaps he's . . . well perhaps he's back there
now.'

'Yes, I'm sure he's around somewhere. We'll see you tonight
then. Eightish, OK? Bye now.' She paused only a moment as the
line went dead. The dough had glued her hand to the receiver.

Ring Ring. Ring Ring.

A podgy hand with chipped purple nail varnish reached ner-
vously for the phone with the yellow plastic band. No one there.

The green-banded phone.

'Hullo, Nick Farquerson's office.'

'Paula, hello, Jocelyn here . . . is . . .'

'This isn't Mr Farquerson's assistant actually. Actually she's not here.' The flat nasal voice now was obviously not Paula. Paula sounded languid and sexy on the phone. This voice was both cocky and nervous. And there was the faint rhythm of gum being chewed.

'Oh, who's that then? This is Mrs Farquerson. I wanted to speak to Paula. Is she around somewhere?'

'Well, I don't know. I'm Mavis. I'm just a temp actually. But her coat's not here. Actually she's probably still at lunch.'

'Nick's not by any chance there himself is he?'

'No, I think he went out. His coat's not here.' She chewed some more and thought slowly—'But I sort of remember he said he'd be in the cutting room actually.'

'Yes, of course, the cutting room. I knew that. I knew he would be. I just wanted to remind him to get Jason's present. To remind Paula really. Jason's our son. He's four next week. Do you have the number of the cutting room?'

Ring Ring. Ring Ring.

Paula heard it along the corridor and flung herself through the door in time to forestall Mavis. It was 3.30 after all. She talked through the tangled mohair as she removed a gigantic pink poncho.

'Nick Farquerson's office.'

'Paula, this is Tristram. Where's Nick, for God's sake? I've been after him for over an hour. It's urgent.'

'Is it? What is?' The poncho had draped itself across the floor and onto the chair. Paula perched on the desk stroking the folds from her velvet trousers. She stroked her clothes and through them her body, smiling quietly. Round her neck hung a collar of beaded latticework made by the natives of the Seychelles.

'Look, for Christ's sake! Nick can't just go off like this. He's wanted upstairs. Instanto. Top floor. The press have rumbled the story of this tart who's been taping the shipbuilding deals while sleeping around British Steel. They'll scoop us or stop us. Upstairs are coming on heavy. Where in hell is he?'

Paula chewing on a strand of bleached hair. She answered patiently and deliberately. 'Nick has been buying his son's birthday present, Tristram.'

'Oh, yes. Has he indeed? That's his story I suppose and he's sticking to it!'

'It *is* his son's birthday next week, Tristram. That's a fact. I thought he was your godson?'

'Paula—look, be helpful eh?'

'He said he'd be half an hour after me. So he won't be long now.'

'Thanks—and get him to ring me at once.'

'I will, Tristram.'

'Oh, and Paula. Emma and I are going there to dinner tonight. We'd forgotten about Jason. You couldn't be a sweetie and pop out and get something?'

'Yes, Tristram, of course I will. Don't worry about that side of things at all. I'll see to it later.'

She smiled complacently about herself and her hand in things. And hung the pink poncho on the back of the door.

Ring Ring. Ring Ring.

He counted the times it rang. Usually he only waited five times. This time he drummed his finger on the coin box. He wasn't taking chances—either Jocelyn was in or out. He'd wait. He had his only 10p poised. As the receiver lifted, it went in.

'Hello: 246-8070.'

'Hello. Joss, it's me.'

'Nick—what is it? No one knows where you are!'

'I'm just calling to be sure—anything extra for tonight . . .'

'Like what, Nick?'

'Fetta, olives. Everything OK?'

'Nick, where are you?'

'The cutting room, of course. Like I said. Everything's fine then, is it?'

'The cutting room? Have you been there long?'

'Joss, I told you, lovely, all day. I'll see you about 6, hmm?'

'Nick, are you sure? Are you telling . . .'

'I'll be back in . . .'

Suddenly they were interrupted by what sounded to Jocelyn like the sound of telephone pips. And faintly from Nick, 'Oh Christ . . .'

'Nick where are you? Why are you . . . ?'

But the telephone noises were left hanging in her ear. Jocelyn's mouth tightened. Then slow and purposeful, without placing the receiver back in its cradle, she dialled straight back and got put through.

Ring . . . ring . . . ring . . . It was the extension.

'Hello. 4698.' It was the abrupt surly voice of a man not used to being interrupted.

'Oh hello, is that the cutting room 497?'

'Yes.'

'I'm awfully sorry to interrupt. I wouldn't be calling if it wasn't rather urgent. This is Jocelyn Farquerson. I wanted to have a quick word—just for a second—with my husband. Won't take a minute.'

'Nick Farquerson's not here.'

'Oh, he's editing all day. He just this minute said . . .'

'I don't care what he said. He's not here.'

'Oh, hasn't he been . . . I mean wasn't he . . . ?'

'Look. He left about 12 this morning, and told me he won't be back today. Is that clear?'

'Oh really. He said that. Yes, I see. Thank you.'

Jocelyn stood for a long moment this time. Then went back to the kitchen. A salt tear joined the oil and lemon juice in the bowl of *taramasalata*.

She mustn't jump to conclusions. There had to be another explanation. Just because she and Nick had once used their lunch hours. When she was Tristram's secretary they'd sneaked off sometimes for a couple of hours at a time. To Tristram's London flat. He'd lent them the key. Emma didn't come up to town often. Tristram would change the sheets before she did. There'd been a sort of sexy complicity about it all. They'd giggled over it together. Especially when Nick was making the documentary about adultery as a safety valve on marriage. *The Fidelity Threshold*, it was called.

'Should be a whole section on office adultery,' Tristram had said—'How about the field-work, Joss?'

The men had snorted. But she hadn't found it funny. Their affair was different—a matter of love. Nothing seedy about them at all. And it had certainly proved no safety valve on Nick's marriage. His wife had found out from a forgotten letter. Nick had allowed her a fit of hysterics, a bout of aggrieved sulking and finally, a generous divorce plus maintenance and custody of the two children. Now she lived with them in a council flat in Streatham and belonged to the local One-Parent Family Group. Perhaps Nick would make a documentary about them one day. After all, the field-work was already done.

Here she was suspecting, imagining all sorts of things. The trouble was she knew the scene from inside. She knew the lot of seduced secretaries, the heartbreak of rejected researchers, the emotional debris of this, television's most prestigious department. The department that had accused school assemblies of religious brainwashing, had challenged overspending on the Royal corgis, and had, even now, ready for transmission at peak viewing time, an exposé of the sexual kickbacks in the current ship-building deals. Their public stance was of an unassailable moral rectitude. What they did in their lunch hours was their own affair. And their wives'. Jocelyn reached again for the phone. Then, instead, she did a very unusual thing. She backed the Renault out of the car-port and drove resolutely towards television's Richmond House.

Nick swung into his office exactly thirty-two minutes behind
Paula. They'd synchronised watches in bed over a lingering
cigarette. As he entered she put through the call to Tristram
without so much as a blink—or a complicit smile. It wasn't a
matter of love for Paula.

Tristram's secretary put through the call with crisp efficiency
and a raised eyebrow. Tristram took it with the confidence of the
moral as well as professional upper hand.

'Tristram, I'm here. Sorry I was out.'

'Yes, well you're pushing your luck, old chum. I didn't give
you the key of the flat to use any time you just . . .'

'Yes, I understand. But today . . . well I do appreciate what
you say. You're very kind to . . .'

'That's nothing. But Emma's up in town tonight. So I hope
you've left . . . well anyway. The sixth floor want you. Can you
be in Graham's office by four?'

'Yes, right. Can you make it too?'

'Sure, I'll be there. We need to fight them off, I think, before
it goes even higher. Talk about it on the way up there. But that
other thing. Are you sure everything's OK? I spoke to Joss.
She was after you.'

'Was she? When was that? Did you say . . . ?'

'No, of course I didn't. I'm not stupid. I didn't want to make
things worse.'

'Worse? They're just fine, Tristram; never been better.' Paula
winced but didn't look up. 'Anyway I've spoken to her since.'

'Since?'

'From the cutting room, that is. Yes, and we're both looking
forward to seeing Emma. Joss has concocted this Greek meal;
there's a retsina I've . . .'

'Nick, you weren't in the cutting room—and you're avoiding
the issue.'

'There isn't an issue. Tristram, now for Christ's sake lay off,
will you!'

The meeting on the sixth floor was well under way as Jocelyn strode towards her former office. On the drive in, her anger had hardened as her doubts dispersed. There could only be one explanation. She twice crashed the gears in her impatience, then parked with a squeal of rubber opposite a traffic island, defying, even courting, damage from passing lorries. Let him pay for the repairs. Nothing would please her more. She had given up a steady income and a place where things happened, when she married. She would see about that.

Office doors stood open along the corridors. The rooms listened. Inside, coloured postcards chequered felt notice-boards: foreign beaches from holidaying secretaries, Italian churches from researchers. The colours of patchwork skirts, dun corduroy, exhausted denim swam at the corner of her eye. She strode purposefully. The door to Nick's office said 'No Entry' and referred callers to the next one along. Paula was sitting back at Jocelyn's former desk, biting into a huge and sugary Chelsea bun. She didn't have to worry about her figure—and sex made her hungry. At a smaller desk Mavis chipped more purple from her finger nails.

'Joss— Hello! Come in.' Jocelyn was already in. 'Nick's not here at the moment. In fact he's been out of the office most of the day.' The sight of Paula, the familiarity of a former friend, the suspicion of a new enemy drained Jocelyn of words but not of indignation. She moved towards Nick's private office.

'I want to see him.'

'It's crisis day, I'm afraid. He's in a meeting on the top floor right now. You can wait if you want. Like some tea?'

'Yes, please. And I'll have it in Nick's office.'

'Bun? Cake? Biscuit?' Paula sent Mavis to forage for the canteen trolley now doing its afternoon rounds. Jocelyn took the fetched tea into the inner sanctum and closed the door.

She moved with the precision of controlled anger. It was not a big room; long between door and window, but scarcely more than a desk in width. Nick had sought to invest his tiny space with the overwhelming stamp of his unique identity. The result was much like all the others: a frayed Grotowski poster, in Polish, from his days in Arts Features, a scurrilous attack on Justice Parker hot from the anti-Windscale presses, and the bric-à-brac of his professional ego displayed with an air of self-effacing conceit. Jocelyn knew it all. And began.

First the photographs, the obligatory spread of wife and child, a television man's witness to both domestic bliss and camera expertise. Hers had been taken on one of their stolen weekends, the time when Pat's mother was dying. Nick had caught her—on his Hasselblad, with the wind blowing her hair across her face and she laughing. 150mm lens, 60th at f16. Jason's was of him throwing a beach ball twice his size—shutter speed 500th at f8. She extracted each from their frames, tore them into pieces onto Nick's desk, then wrenched the expensive frames across until the wood cracked and split. Next the prints on the walls: expensive West End lithographs with prestigious names, Prockter, Hockney, Hughes. With the heavy onyx ashtray (a gift from her mother and an acknowledged joke) she smashed the glass, tore out the prints and added their shreds to the pile. The posters joined them. Her sense of exhilaration grew. She seized the long stem of the paper knife and looked round for a further victim. Ever since his programme on meditation Nick had kept a tape recorder and earphones beside him, for silent but inspirational listening to Eastern ragas. She made short work of the earphones, pulping their plastic earmuffs, before gouging into the wired intricacies of the machine itself. Its brittle innards soon spilled across the floor.

Next the book cases: an exclusive array assembled from the costlier of publishers' handouts, and occasional signed volumes from interviewed novelists—on Christian name terms of course. 'It was fun, Beryl.' 'In all thanks and eternal devotion, Edna.' Tristram's own slim volume *The Morality of Media* was among them. Jocelyn yanked not merely the autographed pages but the texts too from their bindings, scattering them across the olive green carpet.

Next, 'hospitality'. Official alcohol started at Tristram's level, but she knew Nick kept a bottle of scotch in a cupboard. Slowly she distributed its contents into each of the four desk drawers. Papers, notes, files, swam brown and clammy.

On further shelves, arrayed in chronological order, labelled and catalogued, were video cassettes of all Nick's best programmes. She had done it herself as an act of love when she was his secretary. Now she undid it, taking them one by one: the promising starters, the well-reviewed, the award-recommended, and the one honoured by BAFTA. Unspooling the black video-tape from each cassette she danced round the room lacing the tape up and down, over and round desk, lamp, chairs, until the whole room looked like some Satanic party decked with black streamers. Jocelyn stood back and warmed with pleasure at the sight. And now the precious award itself. The green bronze half face mounted on its pedestal—nonchalantly placed to be perpetually in his eyeline. It was heavy: it wouldn't break. She stood well back and heaved with all her strength.

The plate glass window seemed to take hours to shatter. She watched its slow-motion collapse from the first crack of impact to the shimmering tinkle of its tiny fragments. Then she took a pen and wrote with a firm hand on Nick's blotter: 'Tristram and Emma arrive at 8. See you then.' And left the room.

Paula and Mavis were facing the door as she came out. For a moment no one moved. Slowly Paula's face broke into a broad grin: 'I'll tell Nick you called.'

'Thanks, Paula. And I'll expect him for dinner. You know how things are.' Paula did. Down the corridor faces had come to the open doors, but no one spoke or intercepted her. She felt as a bride must feel sweeping down the aisle as all heads turn and eyes follow her respectfully round. But she'd married Nick in a registry office. She peeled a parking ticket with satisfaction from the car's windscreen. Then drove home with precise calm, parked with care, let herself into the still house. Ring, ring . . . ring, ring. In the kitchen she resumed supper. Ring, ring—stirring mor oil into the *taramasalata* with a quiet and fierce satisfaction. Ring, ring . . . ring, ring.

PAUL JENNINGS

Cosmo Knight and the Love-Feast

For the third time in a mile Cosmo Knight swung his car
through a ninety-degree left turn and drove about twenty yards
to a ninety-degree right turn. There was no house or tree, nor
even a ditch, to explain why the road did this, why it did not
simply run straight as a die across the undifferentiated fields of
eastern England to the sea, which he was now nearing.

Faced with these arbitrary twists in softer, richer, more
wooded western counties, Cosmo had always had a generalised
picture of peasants, at a period somewhere between the open-field
feudal system and the enclosed farming of the eighteenth century,
shouting under a great oak tree, before some clerkly figure seated
at a table; they were arguing about whose field the road should
skirt and whose it should bisect, and the whole thing was being
written down in a Latin oddly dotted with non-Latin words:
Goodman Jenkyn, Six Mile Bottom, hundred, coppice, dyke. But could
there ever have been peasants, bustling life, in these solitary parts?

To Cosmo this region had a looking-glass air of reversal and
soundlessness. London was real enough, he was real enough. *And
here is Cosmo Knight in another edition of Curious Camera, your programme of world news and views.* You, your, they always said.
Television was real, too: the supreme, universal vocative. You
could look into the camera and stare straight into the eyes of ten
million real people (or so the ratings said); far more than the
entire population when those peasants were here, arguing about

roads, forming the language, forming England.

Suppose it were even more real. Suppose a heraldic king stared into the camera, saying *O people, O England, I am you, I love you. Do this. Do that. Here is what you must do*? Too late. Someone must say that to the whole world now. Suppose a strange announcer with a face of grave and terrible beauty said *O people, switch off your sets. Go out and look up at the night sky and there you will see what you have always known, an Angel, preoccupied*?

Whatever the real effect of this would be in the great meaning-less cities, here on this quiet side of England nothing would happen at all, everything would be turned into silence. Roaring Norsemen had landed here to burn monasteries and rape women, and had instantly vanished into this looking-glass silence. You couldn't place peasants called Goodman Jenkyn here. Only stark figures, Harald, Urk, Aarvold, Jark, in an empty landscape.

He was driving in the general direction of Holland, and there was a pink, vaporous luminosity in the air like that in pictures by Ruysdael; and yet there was this *reversal*. Every Englishman auto-matically thinks of the sun as sinking over the sea. Those English-men who had carried the seeds of Europe over the world, helping in that pollination from which huge, unpredictable flowers were still now bursting out of enormous buds, had sailed west or south. But here the sunset was beginning to form behind him over the land. To the vague pale waters of the North Sea, England presented this silent and unconscious side; a reversal and paradox.

Cosmo was on his way to speak at the annual dinner of the Customs and Excise at Eastport. He had accepted the invitation more or less at random. Every week a score or so of the letters he received were from people asking him to open fêtes and bazaars; and to speak to rotary clubs, soroptimist clubs, undergraduate clubs, men's clubs, women's clubs, literary clubs, political clubs, debating societies, schools; and of course to annual dinners. He was never quite sure whether they asked him because they really thought he would bring them genuine light and information on the Middle East, the Green Pound, stage nudity, the avant-garde

French circus, or on any of the topics for which he was link-man, interviewer of politicians, introducer of little pieces of film; or whether they simply wanted to crowd round and touch him with their fingers, to savour the super-reality of a television personality.

Answering their letters, the mere repetitive act of polite refusal had made these societies and their secretaries seem unreal. In the early days of the programme he had dictated individual replies, but gradually a stereotyped form had evolved, and now there was something simply known to his secretary as the No Letter. *Thank you so much for your kind invitation, but I am very much afraid I cannot accept it. I have a particular interest in your kind of society and I only wish I could come and show the admiration I have for people who don't simply stare at television (even Curious Camera!), but turn out to meetings and take a live interest in affairs. But a visit to (   ) would mean at least a day out of an already crowded week. I do hope you will understand. Yours sincerely.*

Partly from a faint guilt at this mass-produced personalisation, partly from a periodic desire to go and see if it was still really true, that there were people out there, he would accept an invitation once a month or so. In a way it seemed unfair to, for instance, a northern university that had written six times in three years. He had never been approached by Customs and Excise men before, and here he was, instantly accepting their invitation.

Well, it was impossible to please everybody. And he had never been to Eastport, never spoken to Customs men, only been spoken to by them. There is something very *definite* about Customs men, they are the hard real edges of a country. They are the first point at which the real oddness and difference of a nation flower into a uniform, a parade of otherness. Once you get past Customs men you can live in a country, meet the people, learn their language, make friends, eat, possibly marry. You will get to know all the inhabitants before you know the Customs men behind their uniformed masks, their formal assertion of a national separation.

Would they be real here too, in this back-to-front, mirror

landscape where the sunset was wrong, where, instead of the left-hand side (usually the unconscious, feminine, receptive one) England presented her right-hand side to Europe, in that passive silence before she, having absorbed invaders and ideas, turned herself to the world as herself, new, different?

Cosmo stopped the car and wrote on the back of an envelope: *classical Rome, thesis. Gothic north, antithesis. England, synthesis.* No, come, there would be no point in talking about the dialectic to Customs men. Only an after-dinner speech anyway, not a lecture. Jokes. Jokes about *duty*? (*Stern daughter of the voice of God.*) Perhaps joke about huge Customs feast—so *that's* what they do with it all, give huge banquets every year from stocks of wines and foods confiscated from smugglers? Rich meats, exotic contra-band sausages. Their women bedecked with smuggled jewels, wearing three diamond watches each, dressed in cloth-of-gold saris?

No. Customs men would think he was mocking them. Beware of jokes. Beware of jokes *always*.

He had stopped on the brow of a low rise. If you were thirty feet up in this landscape you could see for miles. He got out and stared into the pale fag-end of the sunset, searching for the neutral grey strip that would be the sea. But it was not yet visible. Even here the sea, as on other English coasts, was kept as a surprise, you never saw it until you turned the last corner. Trees, hedges, houses, little ornamental parks went right up to it. The seaside towns, geometrical, anfractuous, went about their business of being land and nurturing irrational human life immediately, from the very shore inwards. And inland the more diversification, the more bends in the road, the longer deferred the moment of meeting the sea (that great nothing and great reality) the better.

From the rise, however, there was visible half a mile away a tubular iron railway bridge and a small town, a huddle of houses crowned by a steeple. This was Debbage, and the bridge was over tidal water. It was still three hours to the dinner, and Eastport was only ten miles further on. He had left London too early:

once you were free of its traffic there was nothing in these flat fields to slow down a journey.

Debbage seemed to be thinking quietly to itself. Cosmo parked his car by a vacant site where, in front of a house literally falling down (the war? Or had the people simply gone away?), with someone's choice in striped blue bedroom wallpaper exposed to the damp sky, there was a notice on the wall saying STATIC WATER TANK 20,000 GALLS. He hadn't seen one of those since London was dotted with them in the days of the fire bombs.

He was out of cigarettes. He went into a little low shop crammed from floor to ceiling with sweets of all kinds, in boxes, tins, jars, silver paper, cardboard packs, Cellophane bags and wrappers. Here was every possible conjunction of sugar with nuts, butter, cocoa, liquorice, coffee, cinnamon, peppermint, caramel, the juice of fruits, gelatine, nameless chemicals and colouring agents; every conceivable variation of succulence, in every shape and colour, that would fit into the human mouth; a child's dream of sucking made into a huge and serious adult business. These things were produced by intricate, quick-moving machines in vast factories, brought here by train and lorry in unimaginable prodigies of organisation (and there must be sweet *salesmen* too. *Now here's something very special, Mrs Potts. Our new line. Nutty Scrumpo. Try it. Mmmm*). Why was it deserted, why were there no Debbage people in the shop, plunging their arms eagerly into this miraculous cornucopia so splendidly poured out into their dull, glucose-starved lives beside this muddy river?

As he pocketed his twenty Players and turned to leave, the shop bell tinkled and a grizzled man with steel-rimmed glasses entered. 'Are you Mr Cosmo Knight?' he asked.

Just like anywhere else; they didn't mend their nets here or sing sea shanties, they watched the television, as in London or Birmingham. But the man did not ask for his autograph. He said, 'You dropped this,' and gave Cosmo the envelope bearing his name, on which he had written *Classical Rome, thesis, Gothic north, antithesis. England, synthesis.*

'No money in it, ha ha,' said the grizzled man.

Cosmo went down a side street and paused to light a cigarette in front of a shop window full of trousers, oilskins, sweaters, knives, rope, paraffin lamps, bicycle pumps. Across the road a brass plate on a blank-looking house, inside which a telephone was ringing, said OCULIST. Suddenly there were people in the street, coming towards him from both ends: two women with babies in push-chairs, a man in a mackintosh, an old woman, a youth on a bicycle, like Pirandello characters in this absurd street. They couldn't all be non-television-viewers, like the grizzled man. Feeling foolish, Cosmo went into the trouser shop.

He thought wildly. A knife? A primus stove? A tarpaulin of some sort? Anything but a pair of those thick trousers.

'I'd like to see some undervests,' he said. A man appeared from behind a library of trousers arranged on shelves. He breathed heavily. From another shelf he took down a box containing undervests of pure wool. They bore no trade mark of any kind and were tied together in bundles of six. They were undoubtedly new, in the sense of unused, but there was a pre-war look about them, or perhaps they were the kind issued to the police and firemen. They were much heavier than what Cosmo normally wore, but it might be useful to have a couple of pairs in stock, perhaps for bitterly cold days when celebrities had to be interviewed at airports.

The man, not uttering a word, wrapped them up. The street was empty again. As Cosmo was going out the man said, 'I hope you don't mind my asking you, Mr Knight, but my boy would be so pleased if I could have your autograph.'

'Would *you* be pleased?' said Cosmo.

'Well, probably more pleased, in the sense of valuing it,' said the man, 'He's only seven. You couldn't really ask him to appreciate your programme, like the one about the Common Market. But they swap autographs, you know. I expect two of yours is worth one pop singer's. Oh yes, quite a rate of exchange. No offence, you know. Very interested to meet you. You haven't got to buy those vests if you don't want 'em, you know.'

'What do *you* think of the Common Market?'

'Well, I think of the Chinese, and all the Africans and Indians. And sometimes I see one of these American bombers, they fly over the coast here, going east. And I think, What's he got in there, I hope he knows where to turn back. And I think of the Russian ones turning back, over Poland. And somehow I can't give my mind to the Common Market. Although of course I hope those Germans *are* different now. If I was the United Nations, I'd try to get a law, everybody must marry a foreigner.'

'Then we'd all be Chinese.'

'No, you work it out. They're only seven hundred out of more than two thousand million. Have a programme about it, I don't mind, you know.'

The telephone was still ringing in the oculist's house as Cosmo drove on. Who could possibly want an oculist as urgently as that, why not leave it till tomorrow if he was so obviously out? Cosmo imagined someone, in a dark house on the marshes, praying, cursing, sobbing over the telephone, while upstairs, in an old high bedroom, someone else lay dying, the only person in the world able to decipher a vital document—an ancient text that could change and save the world, a formula, an invention, perhaps for instantly destroying anything of metal once it was five hundred feet above the ground, anywhere—and as the old eyes misted over with death the precious glasses, inadvertently trodden on, lay in useless fragments on the bedside carpet.

Eastport, lit from behind by the declining sun, stood up in clean slabs of colour that seemed at once pastel and poster. It had the slightly mad super-reality of a sea town, as strange to natives approaching it from the land as to strangers coming on it from the sea. The hotel booked for Cosmo was one of many such in England, with a lot of cream-painted woodwork, many little carpeted corridors, a small lounge with easy chairs that had curved wooden arms, where people sat having tea or coffee in whispers. But here the guests had a faintly puzzled and expectant look, as though they had been to many hotels but could now go no further and must stop here to face some sort of actual life, possibly even together, as a body. There was an atmosphere of complicity, they stared when Cosmo entered a room. It might have been because of the television; but none of them asked for his autograph.

He rang a bell. It was answered by the standard waiter in such hotels, an Irishman of forty or so with a keen face and soft eyes, wearing a short white jacket.

'I'd like some tea in the writing-room.'

'Very good, Mr Knight,' said the Irishman confidentially, 'I'll see no one disturbs you.' How would he do that, Cosmo wondered? Tell noisy-looking people the writing-room was closed for redecoration? Lock the door? Actually sit in there like a librarian and tell people to be quiet?

There was no one else in the writing-room. Cosmo poured out a cup of tea and began to write steadily on the hotel note-paper.

'Customs and Excise men. This is an extraordinary and historic night. This big quiet sky, this wide empty sea, this actual place of Eastport, this moment, this gathering here, is the electrode and arc-point from which an enormous voltage of love and reason, which has for years been gathering head everywhere, will suddenly emit a blinding discharge of light that will utterly fuse, unify and change the world. We, my brothers, have been chosen for this, here in the quietest part of England, England that is between Germany and France, between north and south, between east and west, between ancient and modern. Let your hearts burst with joy now that the long unreality is over; for here is the joy of reality, the only reality, that we are all men.

'You have been chosen for this sacrificial gesture of utter change from within. I see from the lines of thought and suffering on your faces, you beloved Customs men, who have loved your sweet wives in the night, who have marvelled at the infinite question in the eyes of your babies, that you have all hoped for this, hoped that life was not simply to be increasingly unreality for ever. Heroically you have struggled to hold on at this point where Fate has placed you, between the past and future.

'Your whole being as Customs and Excise men is rooted in the past, the past of nations forming themselves over slow centuries of bullock carts, the growth of temples and languages, of cities and armies. I, with this message from the future, am as English as you, I know how you have searched your hearts to see what could be done that was not in terms of that past. You will all have said to yourselves, in the lonely night hours when you yourselves are the only occupants of the Customs sheds (those great prisons of the past), *fifty million Englishmen, ninety-three thousand square miles; forty million Frenchmen, two hundred and ten thousand square miles; a hundred and eighty million Americans, three million square miles; seven hundred million Chinese* . . . and you will have wondered whether you dare say *one baby in one mother's arms.*

'You will have heard bombers not yours whine high over Eastport, you will have read of rockets not from your past. And you will have turned again, with a sigh, to the traveller now standing before you and shown him yet again, the List of Contraband Articles.

'You Customs and Excise men, I come to you from a future where there are no Englishmen, no Americans, no Chinese, no Russians, only men, their wives, their babies. Rejoice now, put off doubt, let us announce joyfully to the world that Customs are absurd, the past is over.

'But, my brothers, in the flush of this joy let us not forget we are still men living in time and space, requiring practical organisation and deeds; it is because of this that I bring you from the volatile regions of the air and television to the practical and mothering sea, bearer of solid cargoes, womb of us all. Let us now, this very night, take over the boat that lies in the harbour, as the first of a mighty fleet of joy. We will sail to other ports in other lands where their Customs men will give dinners such as this to us; great international love-feasts of Customs men; for the news of our action, here this night at Eastport, will have flashed across the world. And it will spread, like a rapid fire from the Customs

men to the nations behind them, the people will line the quay-side
for us, calling out in soft musical voices, waiting with girls and
flowers. For once reality is taken away from these formal dykes,
built up in the past, between nations; once you yourselves, in a
voluntary motion of pure love, have abjured the uniform which,
in the past, has been a more positive sectional statement than that
of any soldier (for even soldiers assume that the war will end
some day, but until this glorious night everyone thought Customs
go on for ever)—once this first gesture is made, the soft amor-
phous masses of people behind you, ready for love, will easily
coalesce and flow together.

'Even the strongest governments, living in the past, well
accustomed to dealing with mere military or naval mutinies, will
be nonplussed by action from this unexpected quarter. They will
not dare to take violent measures against you for fear of looking
absurd: it would be as unforgivable as massacring all their post-
men. And while they are wondering what to do, other Customs
men of the world will be joining us in other boats. You and they
will bring your unmarried sons and daughters; and with the
support of the United Nations we shall begin to build up the
great International Marriage Fleet.

'There may be initial hardships. There may be confusion over
your actual jobs and livelihoods during the transitional period,
before the vast organisation of the International Marriage Fleet
absorbs not only you but thousands more in profitable and con-
structive employment. There may even be violence and death.
But do not, on this happy night, let this obscure from you the
wonderful nature of what is happening here, why only you can
do this thing that will save the world. They will see that this is
no mere local Customs Union or hard-won grudging reciprocal
agreement painfully reached by suspicious governments, but a
total bursting of the bonds of the past, a spontaneous welling up
of love, the unifying of man. Onward, beloved Customs and
Excise men, onward, to the sea and the world.'

Cosmo became aware of voices raised in argument at the door

of the writing-room. 'I'm sorry, Mr Rostrevor,' said the Irish
waiter, 'Mr Knight is writing and must not be disturbed.'

'Damn it, Paddy,' said a masterful voice, 'he's speaking at our
dinner and it starts in ten minutes.' The speaker, a big plum-
coloured man in a tuxedo, came in, shook Cosmo's hand, and
led him towards the bar through a crush of Customs men and
their wives, all in evening dress, saying as he did so, 'Ah, good,
thought you weren't coming, you television chaps, care to join
the committee, in the bar, like to introduce you, Mr Hope, our
treasurer, Mr Wallaby, Mr Pope, Mrs Cope, hello Jack, mumble
mumble, yes, yes, tell them it's all right, see you after, Mr Pope,
Mrs Wallaby, press are here, they want a photograph, well, Mrs
Pope here, on the other side, you here, yes,'. He seemed to end
on a comma.

'Would you smile at Mrs Cope, Mr Knight,' said the photographer. All photographers can make you feel amateur, thought
Cosmo. He began to gabble to the little bespectacled woman
dressed in lace at his side. 'What a curious part of England, I've
never been here before, one doesn't somehow expect to find Customs men at the end of these fields.'

Mrs Cope looked up at him owlishly. 'Are you from the television? We had Sir Harold Carter last year.' At last the flash went,
the group broke up. A pretty, lively, dark-haired girl, about six
months pregnant, came up to him and said, 'We're dying to hear
you. I always watch *Curious Camera*, you're my favourite man on
TV, would you mind signing this?'

'This is Mrs Wallaby,' said Mrs Cope.

'Who is Sir Harold Carter?' said Cosmo to the girl. I wish she
was mine, he thought; and then, No, there are pretty girls everywhere, it's right that a young Customs man, bet he doesn't get
much over three thousand a year, should have one.

'I don't know,' she said. 'We weren't here last year, this is only
John's second place, we came to this dump from Liverpool.'

'Ladies and gentlemen, dinner is served,' shouted the toastmaster in his red tail-coat. He had the violently scrubbed-

looking face of his trade. He drew Cosmo aside and, in a manner somehow both deferential and condescending, began an earnest discussion of the microphone, its placing, where Cosmo would be sitting, how he was to be introduced.

The crowd moved into the dining-room, a later annexe to the hotel with a complicated roof of cream-painted wooden joists, iron tie-rods, glazed and wired sky-lights. It seemed chilly, but of course if it had been warm now it would be only to become stifling after an hour with a hundred people in it.

Cosmo sat at the top table between Mr Rostrevor and Mrs Cope. He passed the meal in the familiar dream situation of the guest whose neighbours each have neighbours on the other side whom they have known for years, and have to keep, whenever they remember, turning from real and particular conversations with them to unreal and general ones with the guest. 'Oh yes, we had Sir Harold Carter last year,' said Mr Rostrevor abstractedly. 'Some of the committee wanted a television personality this year, very good of you to come.'

'They do a very good dinner here,' said Mrs Cope, or Pope. 'Yes, quite a good dinner.'

Outside were marshes and the sea. They drank Pouilly Fuissé and Macon as they worked through Cream of Mushroom Soup, Fillet of Sole with Shrimp Sauce, Roast Saddle of Mutton with Château Potatoes and Garden Peas, Pear Melba, Cheese Straws, Coffee. The room grew very warm.

The toastmaster banged on the table. 'Pray silence for your Chairman, who will give the Loyal Toast.'

'The Queen, the Queen, God bless her, rhubarb, rhubarb,' mumbled the company.

'You have your chairman's permission to smoke.'

'Did you ever hear about the dinner presided over by a very strict old general?' said Cosmo to Mrs Cope. 'They had all been smoking between the courses, and he was furious, but he couldn't stop it. But after he gave the Loyal Toast he said, "*Gentlemen* may smoke. Those who are already smoking may continue to do so".'

'We had a general, General Jones, the year before Sir Harold Carter,' said Mrs Cope in a whisper, for Mr Rostrevor was now introducing Cosmo to the audience.

'. . . of course I don't look at the television myself, but here he is, Mr Cosmo Knight.'

There was a sound of chairs scraping as people turned to face him. A sudden thought shot into Cosmo's head. *Would Mrs Wallaby keep her baby in a pouch?* And then he was on his feet.

'Mr Chairman, ladies and gentlemen,' said Cosmo, 'you are doubtless wondering whether I have anything to declare (*laughter*). I am wondering myself (*laughter*). I will confess to you that if there is one thing that frightens me more than one Customs officer it is a hundred Customs officers (*laughter*) *and their wives*. Everyone knows there are marriage customs, but one does not think so often of Customs marriages (*laughter*). And the only thing that enabled me to overcome this fear was the thought that perhaps I might be the very first non-Customs man to be admitted to your secret rites, to penetrate the mystery of what happens to all the stuff you confiscate (*loud laughter*). Here, I thought, will be an enormous feast, the tables groaning with exotic dishes prepared from such things as 'uncooked meats and non-European rabbits' which I have observed from a Customs notice at London Airport to be prohibited goods. There would be at each gentleman's place a box of the choicest confiscated cigars, and two confiscated gold watches; at each lady's place a diamond necklace. (*Loud laughter. Good, they would take this well*). For the guests, a simple gold brick, perhaps. But seriously, we in television . . .'

Cosmo slipped easily into Speech A, about real people being necessary to television, and the duty of television to keep in touch with the ordinary, real people. Those who keep the wheels of the world turning. He included three very good jokes, ending with the best one, and sat down to standard applause.

MELVYN BRAGG

Towards the Morning

She closed her front door so decisively behind her that she
feared the loud slap of it might wake up the child. She waited,
hoping for a cry which would take her back in to where she was
needed; but it did not come. Joanna was asleep and well and the
neighbour who was baby-sitting was entirely reliable. Gingerly,
like someone crossing stepping stones, Mary went the few yards
from the door to the street. Her garden was parched and bald,
like the rest of them this drought-smitten summer. The street was
empty. There were trees, she knew the place well, they had bought
the house there five years ago, it was a quiet safe street in a
quiet safe part of London and yet as she came through her gate
and heard her high heels strike the pavement, Mary felt im-
prisoned. Only inside the house was she free now. A nauseous
panic rushed into her throat and made her dizzy. She remembered
feeling sick in the car when she was a little girl on Sunday outings.
'Wind down the window and take a deep breath,' her father had
always said. 'Deep—Breath—Deep—Breath— Thaaaat's—it!'
She took a deep breath of the warm heavy evening air. 'Thaaaaat's
it! Feel better?' Yes. Thank you, father, dead.

  She set off for the party. It was only three streets away and the
walk would do her good. The party would do her good. Just to
get out of the house on her own should do her good. The careful
bath, the length of time devoted to making herself up, above all
the determination to face up to their old friends and be seen to

be coping—all that should do her good. She had stayed in the house too long since the rupture, mourning his departure as keenly as if it had been his death. The time had come to make a new start, be brave, get out of herself—all the things her friends said and she agreed. But, God, why, as she, a slim woman in her early thirties, walked, firmly now, through these calm city streets, clear and ordered in her intention, why were the walls of her mind still weeping with fear and loss and regret? She had not known she had loved him so much.

They had assured her that he would not be there. The Stewarts were more her friends than his. It was odd how soon and how easily they had divided up their friends, how effectively he had worked out a zone for himself which was outside her perimeters, how quickly their lives had separated, joined now only by the Sunday afternoon visitation, with presents for his daughter. All in a few months.

The party was in the garden. The Stewarts' place was similar to her own but through painstaking efforts the garden was still green. It was the first thing Mary noticed as she came out of the French windows—the common shiny green of an English lawn somehow exotic, even indecent under the darkening blue early evening sky which looked down on earth baked brown all over the land.

'He does it in the middle of the night,' Alexandra said as she steered Mary by the elbow towards the jovial group clustered around the large dining-table which had been set between the two big chestnut trees like a hyphen. 'He *does*!' Alexandra repeated even though Mary had revealed no surprise; the explanation was part of Alexandra's automatic party line and Mary was relieved because she did not want to have to think either; all her energy was concentrated on keeping herself physically steady as she advanced to the battalion of waiting friends and acquaintances, turning their heads (were they *all* turning their heads?) and baring their teeth in smiles as she came to them like a victim. 'He does a different bit every night with an old fashioned watering can. The hose-pipe would make too much noise, he says, and I'm not sure it's legal—*but*—you won't *believe* this—all the water comes from the *bath*. Yes. We leave the water in the bath and then off he goes with his little tin can—one of those really old fashioned things—and—it's disgusting! You know everybody, I think. Pimms?'

She was welcomed with such finely-tuned sensibilities that she almost burst into tears. No one patronised her, no one bluffly pitied her, no one made cow's eyes of pathos or darted glances of wounding curiosity. They shuffled a little and let her in among them, the cold glass was in her hand and she was talking about the new nursery school in the church hall.

But the relief which came from the conversation lasted only a few minutes. Her full attention was fixed on herself and would not be seduced away. The familiarity of the people and the subjects, the amiable gossip of a group which was held together by similarities of income, education and, perhaps above all, the age of their children, all that heightened villagey-communion which rose, here as elsewhere, apparently so effortlessly, out of the metropolis, even all that shared and sustaining comfort could not do more than provide just another setting for the thoughts that gnawed her spirit. Like a fox in a trap which gnaws off its own leg to be free: that image had occurred to her several times and it stuck in some groove of pain ever ready to spin back into her mind. No, after she had survived the first few minutes, this party at which she had thought to get out of herself had no more effect than changing position in a chair. And so she drifted once more back on to the rocks of her distress.

Later there was some hot quiche lorraine. When she nibbled at her slice, Mary realised how hungry she was. She swallowed two large mouthfuls greedily, but that was enough; as suddenly as her appetite had arisen, it fell away. She could eat no more.

They were sitting higgledy-piggledy about the patio now, looking down the garden to the two proud chestnuts, leaves limp in the still air. Very, very slowly, as if determined to fight every second of the way, the sky yielded its light. An aeroplane ripped across the houses and Mary smiled at the sound.

'Thank God we only get them when the wind's in the east,' Alexandra said, 'or is it the north-east?' She squatted on a small stool, dwarfing it and somehow herself diminished, her buttocks hanging over the edges, her knees touching, feet splayed out, body hunched over the plate of quiche. 'If we were like poor old Kew or *Hounslow*! How *do* they manage?' She smiled up at Mary, who caught that flash of pity until now absent from the evening. She finished her drink rapidly. She drank much more these days.

'Another?' Again that beam of unmistakable sympathy. Mary nodded and tried to pull herself back into the present: she had had enough pity. She must show that she could manage without it. That was the point.

'I might start work again next month,' she said, over-lightly, brittle she knew, but, she urged herself, go on, just go on. 'Yes. Joanna'll be at the nursery school—the new one—Sheila and I were talking about it just now—she'll be there *all* day now—and with Sheila herself working there—that gives me—all day, well not quite, but.' She was speaking more quickly, sipping at the gin-based drink too often, her voice became louder, the words lurched out of her mouth: she could not stop. 'Well, if I can leave at say—say nine—and get there—say—on the tube—nine-thirty—quarter-to-ten—I can—have to—work through lunch—I don't need lunch—and leave at—say two—say two-thirty—two-thirty—getting back at three—well—two-fifteen to get back at three—they said that was more than part-time but just to do *mornings*—somehow—it isn't *like* a job to do just mornings and with that sort of work—anyway—' Another aeroplane went over. Alexandra's hands fled dramatically to her ears and she grinned through the noise—like someone indulging a child or an invalid, Mary thought—no, not that—no—not that. She stood up and was, again, momentarily dizzy.

'I'm late.'

'*Must you?*' There was relief in Alexandra's voice—was there

not? The paranoia came in very like a flood. They were all saying
. . . The whole evening they had really been thinking . . . when
she went . . . No. Not that.

'I said I'd be back by ten-thirty.'

'Nick will run you round.'

'I'd rather walk, really I would, it's the best time of day for a
walk—*please*.' She added that last word desperately as she saw
Alexandra heaving herself up off the stool and visibly gathering
her forces to insist on Mary accepting her generosity. 'Please,'
she repeated, knowing it was a plea and immediately paying the
penalty, for Alexandra nodded so understandingly that there was
a hush on the patio and 'goodbyes' were all, it seemed to Mary,
bandaged with concern.

On the still street again, walking quickly home.

He was watching television, in the dark, one leg dangling over
the side of the big armchair, posed, she thought, or sulky—but
those reflections were the merest vestiges of objectivity, futile
tribute to self-restraint, straws thrown down to stop the flood as
the dam burst and she ran to him, high heels cracking loudly on
the wood-blocked floor and fell into his lap, keening.

'Hey now,' he said, gently, stroking her hair with the old
gesture. 'Hey now.'

The keening in its first moment had something of the ridiculous
in it, he thought, so canine; and then there was beauty. so ancient.
But it went on, the tears not softening it, the bare sound of soul-
pain, unearthly, and he shifted his position in the armchair,
clumsily trying to jostle her out of it.

'Come on,' he said, still gentle but more urgent now. 'Come
on now. Sweetheart. Oh?'

At the word 'sweetheart' she stopped and pulled away from
him, holding his gaze with a look of such deliberate intensity that
he was trapped into returning it. So they stared, eye-locked, and
again he soon put aside all light-hearted remarks which might
occur to him about this mesmeric connection: her seriousness
sliced through his well-developed front of easy-going worldliness

as heavily as an axe through a piece of kindling wood. It had always been like that and he was filled with awe and dread.

Still she held his look and his mind emptied, the warm balm of the night seeping into it with protective drowsiness. And then she smiled, the lovely smile entrancing on her thin, hurt face.

'You *do* love me,' she said and leaned forward to kiss him briskly like a sister. 'Don't you?'

He could neither confirm nor deny it. To confirm it would be to ignite again what had taken such efforts to dampen and defuse; to deny it would be to hurt her unforgivably at what was plainly a most fragile moment. And there was no answer in a more profound sense because he *did* love her. There had been a real conjunction, sensual, enjoyable, intense, friendly, and such few loves as those took captive part of your affections for ever. Yet he did not want to live with her. As she saw it, though, real love involved total commitment and there was no way in which she could square the circle as he so successfully (and sometimes he thought in self-disgust, superficially) could seem to do.

His answer was a cowardly sigh leaving her to interpret it.

'Of course you do,' she said, bravely, and they both heard the hopelessness fall between them like a coin dropped into a deep well; and waited now for it to strike the earth.

But she had much more energy than that, she had the vibrancy of despair and she grasped the moment fiercely.

'Scotch?' She leapt from his knee, knocked off the television and whirled round in the murky light. 'Oh! You let Lena'—the neighbour who had been baby-sitting—'go home?'

'Yes.'

'So you must have been waiting for me,' Mary concluded slyly, and put on a small table light in the corner of the room which became soft and romantic in the way Mary most loved.

'Well?' she pressed him. 'You must have been.'

'I knew you wouldn't be too late back from Alexandra's,' he said dryly, knowing that he was being ungallant but using the opportunity to reassert his independence.

Mary hopped over the snub to root out the more important part.

'How did you know I *was* at Alexandra's?'

'They asked me, too.'

She felt that spin of fear again, that sudden steep chasm in the mind, as barrel spun around and the bullet was seen to be lodged ready for firing.

'But they told me . . . I thought *you* . . .'

'Alexandra was trying to be kind,' he said cruelly. 'You know her. I was supposed to turn up "accidentally on purpose".'

'I can't trust her any more,' Mary said, pathetically.

He had gone too far and corrected his mistake as expertly as a yachtsman at the tiller.

'Don't be silly,' he said breezily, 'she was just trying to help. You know old Alex-plonk-plonk-heavy-feet but heart of gold.'

'Scotch?'

'Come on, Mary, don't cut Alex off just like that. She's a decent woman.'

'You never liked her.'

'That's not the point.'

'What is?'

'She's a decent woman. When people are decent and serious—okay they make mistakes. But you can't just dismiss them if they blunder a bit.'

'Don't be so pious!'

'Sorry.'

'No you're not.'

'I am. I am sorry, Mary, I *am*!'

'Are you?' The question was innocently voiced, her eyes were misty. The aggression had drained out of her tone as rapidly as it had invaded it. She stood in a corner of the room like a penitent. 'I'm sorry,' she said, sadly. 'I must believe you.'

'What about you, a Scotch?'

He got up, went across to the drinks, passing her on the way as she stood there still, self-consuming. Two Scotches, topped up with water, no ice; last drink before bed, an old habit, time for the final gossip, the idling chat, the laziness of not yielding to sleep, true intimacy.

They sat in their usual chairs.

'Cheers.'

'Cheers.'

And silence.

A Silence which grew and he could not afford that, not in his old house, not with the cossetting dry air of the hot summer, not with the light so and the drinks, and his wounded wife before him, at bay.

'It's taken over,' he said, with a heartiness he loathed, 'hasn't it? Jim Martin was talking about it the other day at the *Statesman*'s do. There's a shop he goes into to buy fags. "Cheers" says the fellow behind the counter when he goes in. Meaning—"Good morning". He asks for 20—Embassy or whatever—"Cheers" the chap says—or rather "Chuss." Meaning—"Yes, I'll get you those" and when he hands them over he says "Cheers" (or Chuss). Meaning—"Here they are". "Cheers" again meaning—"Thank you" when the money is handed over and "Cheers" when the change is given meaning "Here is your change and thank you again." As he goes out, a final "Chuss' meaning—"See you soon" or "Good-bye" or 'Have a good day"—take your pick!' He grinned at her, hoping the badly told story would at least give notice that he was perfectly willing to engage on one level but quite determined to stick to that level.

'Cheers,' he added, very lamely, and took a big drink.

'Why *are* you here, then?' she asked, as ever going for the nerve of the matter.

The temptation to be nice was almost overwhelming: his wish to comfort her, his longing now to help salve the pain he had so much to do with; and he did love her.

'I was passing,' he said, half-truthfully.

Her stillness admonished him.

'I can't come this Sunday,' he said. 'So I came tonight.'

'To see your daughter.' Mary said the words slowly as if spelling them out to an uncomprehending listener.

'Yes,' he confessed and felt simultaneously better and worse for the full truth being flushed into the open.

'She was asleep when I left,' Mary said.

'She was sleeping lightly,' he said. 'I just went up to look at her but she woke up and we played a bit . . .'

'You must have arrived just after I left,' Mary continued. Her head was inclined downwards; she was intent; her line of thought was relentless.

'Yes.' Dry-throated, he finished the whisky but did not feel it would be right at this moment to get another. He had enough respect to obey that intuitive injunction but he longed for another drink and felt parched.

'Did you know at what time I was leaving?'

'Sort of.'

She paused, puzzled at the problem for a moment, and then went forward. 'You didn't watch me leave, did you? You weren't somewhere in the street watching as I left?'

He hesitated: but the issue now held the field and it could not be resisted.

'Yes,' he said.

'Oh!' Her hand swept to her mouth to staunch the cry and she raised her head, and looked at him, waiting.

But he had nothing to add.

'It wasn't me then,' she said, finally, wearily, driving in once again. 'You came to see her, not me.'

'I waited for you,' he replied; it was some sort of comfort, perhaps.

'You had to,' she said, sweeping aside his protestation. 'The baby-sitter had gone home. You had to wait for me.'

He hesitated and then got up and poured himself another, stiffer, Scotch. He turned to her and she held out her empty glass.

'I'll take yours,' she said. He made the exchange and sat down once more, wishing he was gone.

'You want to bugger off now, don't you?' Mary said, crudely.
'No, no, I . . .'
'Bugger off if you want to.'
'I'll finish this drink.'
'You're lucky to get it. The money you give is hardly enough
to eat on. Alan and Sue bought me that.'
'The money thing is the best I can do; it's difficult, Mary . . .'
'Oh—fuck off!'
The language did violence to her. She was so elegant, neat and
careful, and the obscenities were a warning. He knew it well.
'I'll be off,' he said, put down the glass only half drunk, and
stood up, almost jaunty now that it was over.
She would not look up at him and he required to catch her eye
before he left. He could not go without a glance from her—even a
bitter one: the alternative appeared too dishonourable, a cowardly
stealing away. But she would not look up, perhaps aware of the
power this gave her.
'Mary,' he called out gently. 'Mary.'
She did not answer nor did she look at him. He stood there,
helpless. She began to sob, and drawn immediately, he went
across, knelt before her and looked into a face disfigured by
distress.
'I'm sorry,' she said, trying strenuously to subdue her weeping.
'I'm sorry. Going on like this. Just—say goodnight and go—I'll
be fine.' She paused and gathered herself for a last throw. 'Really—
I'll be fine—just—go: just go.'
But he could not go and they slid on to the floor, her weeping
released now, her body clinging to him for some comfort, hope
yet again rising above exhaustion. They made love there on the
floor only half undressed, like guilty schoolchildren. To her 'I
love you' he made no response but he was kind, and she knew
he loved her, she said; he did not have to say so.
He left, after a nicely-judged allotment of time. Mary went into
the garden and sat down on the bare earth, where there should
have been grass.

'Deep breath. Feeling better? Thaaaat's it.'

Towards the morning she grew cold but stayed outside watching the other houses, the few limp trees, the sky. It would be another fine day.

JAN WEBSTER

Abercrombie's Aunt

'People don't have aunts nowadays,' Lulu had said.

What is this advancing towards me in sensible ferry boats and freshly-cleaned circus tent if it isn't an aunt? wondered Abercrombie. The same who had dispatched him south twenty years before, at age sixteen, braces through the loops in his Interlock underpants, four well-smoothed pound notes in a monogrammed wallet, eight clean hankies, his Highers and a Biblical text under his clean copy of *How to Write* by Stephen Leacock.

'What have you got in here?' Her fibre suitcase was dislocatingly heavy and he staggered about the Euston concourse like a manic Max Wall. 'Do you mean to tell me you still go in for those ironclad bloomers that used to festoon the kitchen pulley on wet Mondays?'

'I have a wee minding in there for you.'

'What is it? The Stone of Scone?'

'No. Just home-baked sultana cake. I hope you're not going to talk about knickers in front of your intended,' said Abercrombie's aunt, lemon-mouthed. 'She'll wonder what sort of home you came out of. Where's this So Ho they're always talking about?'

'You wouldn't like it, Auntie.' It was like feeling protective towards HMS Hood or Mick McManus.

'I might not like it, but I could always say I'd been there.' Abercrombie's aunt steered a deliberate course towards the cafeteria. 'Can we not have some tea and a bun or something? I want to discuss things with you before I meet your intended.'

My intended what? wondered Abercrombie gloomily, as he queued with a tray, watching his aunt settle at a table like a carthorse backing into the shafts.

More like my *doomed*. He was perfectly happy with the relationship as it was and now the aunt would want to cross t's and dot i's. He and Lulu after long agonised discussions had decided that out of consideration for his aunt's Presbyterian principles, he would sleep on a camp bed in the living-room for the duration of her visit and Lulu would pretend the box-room was her customary resting place. He felt unreasonably irked to be denied the big bedroom where something unexpectedly good and joyful had been celebrated over the last seven months. But the aunt was the aunt. Jesus and No Quarter.

He would have to try and get her to understand that the relationship between himself and Lulu was an open one that she had no right to try to define or restrict. Looking over at her, he sighed at the near-impossibility of the task. Her recent letters had been heavy with intimations of mortality and prescience of Calls Home. Lulu might not know it, but she was due to be vetted as a vessel for the propagation of the Abercrombie species. Her Upper Second in History would be no protection. He felt a shrinkage in his loins and would not have been too surprised to look down and see red scabby knees above short trousers.

Provincial complexes that had troubled him not at all in recent years rose up to haunt the space behind the café tea urn. The need for Good Behaviour in front of the woman who had sacrificed all to bring him up; to revert to parochial Scot instead of cosmopolitan one. His aunt's burr-y Strathclyde patois had disengaged lever after lever so that the mind sped back to childhood trauma and insecurities.

He'd had someone on one of his recent programmes at the Beeb who'd gone into all that rather entertainingly. One of those young professors in a tweed tie and Red Baron flying jacket, discussing the dual nature of the Northern race, as he saw it torn between nostalgia for The Wee Hoose Amang the Heather and the need to dominate in the south.

Lulu had said with that sharp missionary look of hers that he should explore the dichotomy. He hadn't been all that sure what the word meant until recently, when he'd quietly looked it up, but now that its definition stared him in the face he realised Lulu had been right. Somehow he should have stonewalled the aunt.

Looking at her now, he felt as though his stomach were lined with the dry crumbs of digestive biscuits. Age had attacked that citadel of proletarian rectitude. Flesh was falling in soft, Plasticine folds from the massive, porridge-based frame, loose skin flapped in dewlaps about the formidable jaw. Seeing her raise an arm to wipe her forehead with a freshener pad, he remembered that hand parting and combing his hair with all the gentleness of a combine harvester. She had clicked lights out, refusing to let him read in bed. Made him walk on newspapers across the kitchen floor. Yet the light on her face when he read the lesson in church on his sixteenth birthday had been an awesome sight, winter sun on Ben Nevis. The bloody hat she wore now—surely it had made the trip south five years ago? She usually bought a new hat when she was going somewhere special. Was it too much of an effort these days? Guilt's hag face nodded at him from behind the tea urn.

Abercrombie had sidled into television from journalism just in time, before the postwar Bulge, with their theses on Gramsci and Aspects of the African Novel, descended from the universities and took over. He had always looked better educated than he was. Reithian. 'The perfect media man,' Lulu teased. 'All that breadth and no depth.' 'Send a fool to college,' he retorted, 'and all you get is an educated fool.'

He slopped the tea into the tray, carrying the cups and a Chelsea bun of a particularly revolting yellow towards the aunt, knowing she would stare at it with the disbelief of someone from a region where cakes and tea-bread had been raised to an art-form. Having bought it, he would feel obliged to urge her not to eat it. He felt worn out already. He couldn't cope with two women. It was going to be worse, much worse than he predicted.

'Since you wouldn't bring her up to meet me, I've come down to see her,' said the aunt now without preamble. 'I want to see you settled, Archie. You're thirty-six. I know you say your career comes first, but you'll not be able to warm your feet on your work when you're fifty.'

'Who warmed your feet?' he said, cornered.

'That was no fault of mine. A woman has to wait to be asked.'

'Not any more. Look, Auntie. About Lulu. She's very independent. She knows her way around. Researchers have to be tough, resourceful people.'

'Don't apologise for her.'

'For God's sake, I'm not doing that! I'm just saying: take her as you find her. Don't impose your ideas about marriage and suchlike on her. She won't wear it.'

He had seen that wait-and-see expression on his aunt's face before. Heaving her suitcase, he led the way in the search for a taxi, his expression woebegone and hopeless, that of a man who sees no way out.

'What's this?' demanded Abercrombie's aunt, several hours later. Rushing in from a heavy interview with a Saudi diplomat, Lulu had cooked one of her slapdash but exotic stews.

'Green pepper,' said Lulu.

'Well, if you don't mind, dear, I'll not eat it.' The aunt moved each offending green sliver to the side of her plate. 'It might give me the wind. But the stew's very nice,' she added, generously. 'I can see Archibald has a good wee cook in you.'

'I'm not his cook,' said Lulu pleasantly. 'Nor his bottle-washer, nor his anything else. We go shares.'

'Oh, I know that,' said the aunt innocently. 'Archibald told me. You're an independent wee soul. They make the best kind of wives.'

Abercrombie's eyebrows performed an explicit dance of warning across the table at Lulu. When the aunt had expertly and swiftly tidied up the kitchen and then retired to bed, Lulu exploded.

'I'm not letting this—this charade go on.'

'Ignore her.'

Lulu folded long be-jeaned legs under her and lit a Gauloise. 'No,' she said, decisively. 'She's a woman, like me. A victim of role tyranny. Why shouldn't she go in for a spot of consciousness-raising like the rest of us?'

'Because she's getting on.'

'So what? She's got all her marbles. Underneath all that repression and bigotry, there's a person waiting to be let out.'

He kissed her absently, then protested, 'No. It's—it's a kind of violence, don't you see? Leave her be.'

'Trust me.'

'You're too clever by half. Too bloody consciousness-raised.'

'You hate it because I had a university education and you didn't.'

'I've told you before.' His hand moved inside her blouse. 'We don't get neurotic about education in the north. We're taught to spell and tie our shoe-laces then pointed towards the universe. Best thing.'

As Abercrombie was putting out a programme the next day but Lulu was working on some notes at home, the two women were alone in the Shepherd's Bush flat. 'I'll call you Jean,' said Lulu, spear-heading her attack. 'You are not, after all, my auntie.'

Abercrombie's aunt took in this declaration of intent in silence. She was busy polishing and tut-tutting over the scorch-marked dining-table and setting a trap with cheese for Lulu's tame mouse. The silence built up till Lulu made a pot of tea and, producing the home-made fruit cake, enthused over its flavour and moistness. The aunt's tight mouth relaxed in a careful simper.

'I don't normally like the English,' she confessed. 'But I think maybe you and me'll get on all right.'

'Why don't you like them?' demanded Lulu.

'I once had an English neighbour that never washed her windows nor her curtains.'

'You can't sink much lower than that.'

'That's what I thought. You could hear her laughing and joking on a Sunday and men used to go into her house, with parcels.'

'Parcels?'

'Chocolates and such. One even carried in a bunch of flowers.'

'I sleep with him, you know. Archie.'

The aunt's cup rattled down on its saucer and her mouth fell open, giving her a vulnerable, unprotected look that made Lulu feel, for a moment, the opposite of the parent who said yes, Virginia, there *is* a Santa Claus. Abercrombie's aunt rose and carried her crockery into the kitchen, making a big production out of washing up and putting away.

'Look, I'm sorry.' Leaning against the lintel, Lulu looked it. 'It's just that it—it feels so dishonest, not putting you in the picture. I'm very fond of Archie but I've had other lovers, too. Ever since university.'

If plaid skirts could look flurried, the aunt's did as she marched back into the sitting-room and flopped on the sofa.

'Do I shock you?'

Hands twisted a handkerchief. 'I didn't come up the Clyde on a banana boat,' the aunt protested. 'I knew something was going on.' They stared at each other. 'Don't you *want* to get married? Don't you want to have children?'

'Not yet.'

'Do you love Archie?'

'He's a nice man. A bit of an old woman, in some ways, I suppose because, if you don't mind my saying it, he was brought up by a spinster aunt. I mean sensitive—not effeminate. I like that. It counteracts my boldness. It works.'

'I've never heard the like.' The aunt looked pale, subdued.

Lulu returned to her notes and when Abercrombie came in he looked from one to the other before prescribing large sherries all round.

'Not for me,' said Abercrombie's aunt.

'Drink it up.'

'It goes for my legs.'

'Well, I need one.' He looked beseechingly at Lulu. 'One of the cameras packed up. There was a fight in the hospitality room. Sheeez! I'm glad to be home.'

When Abercrombie looked at his aunt, her glass was empty and there was a flush on her cheeks.

'Give us some home news,' he demanded.

With a smile of bravado she held the glass towards him. 'That's quite a nice harmless wee drink. Give me a spot more and I'll see what I can think of. Oh, yes, I know. You remember Minnie Scoular, her that had the wee Jenny-a'-things shop on the corner? Well, it transpires that she'd been seeing a married man, every Wednesday when she goes into Glasgow, ostensibly to the wholesalers.' She gave Lulu a look that might have been termed triumphant.

'And yon old Wattie Banks? The stories that have been going round about him! She wasn't his wife, you know, that one he had all the sons by. He knocked down a man for saying so, but a chiel came by from Carnwath and he had the right way of it.'

'It sounds a scandalous place, where you come from,' said Lulu softly.

'Well, you see, we have the television and all now. We keep up with the times.'

'Auntie,' said Abercrombie, concernedly. 'You're all right, aren't you?'

'Of course she's all right,' said Lulu. She leaned over and took the hand of Abercrombie's aunt, her gaze soft and even affectionate. 'What was it like when you were growing up, Jean? Were your parents very strict? Did you go to dances? Did they make you work hard?'

'Hard?' Abercrombie's aunt put her other hand over Lulu's. 'Do you know what I'm going to tell you?' Lulu shook her head. 'They made me get up at five in the morning. It was still dark. I had to light the fire, clean the men's boots, make the porridge. I wasn't allowed to eat till everybody else had been seen to. If I protested, my father took the buckle end of his pit belt to me while my mother prayed in a corner. A life?' cried Abercrombie's aunt loudly. 'You ask what kind of life I had. I had no sort of life at all. Work and kirk. Work and kirk. I was a slave. And when I was old enough I put half the county between us. I left them that had shown me no kindness. I got a place of my own and I worked at my dress-making and I never went back.'

'Did you know all this about Jean?' Lulu demanded.

Abercrombie shook his head. 'She would never talk about the family. Would you? All I knew was that after my mother died— and my father who was a soldier in the war—you took me out of it and brought me up as your own.'

'I gave you all I could,' said the aunt. She stared at Abercrombie, then as though wound up began to talk about herself. She described her childhood, her early life in service, the clothes she had made for other people; judiciously, elaborating the bits that took her fancy, refusing to be drawn on other topics. But as suddenly as the flow of anecdote had begun, it ended. 'I'll away to my bed, Lulu,' she said. 'I'm tired.' She put a hand on Abercrombie's face, consideringly, then bent and kissed him. 'Goodnight, Archie son.'

'I've never known her get on so well with anybody,' said Abercrombie two days later. The aunt had been to the Tea Centre with Lulu and in Regent Street had picked a new hat. It was the first he'd ever seen her in without a brim and it suited her. 'It's what you call a toque,' his aunt enlightened him. She preened in front of the mirror.

'I like her,' said Lulu, when Abercrombie's aunt had gone to bed. 'Do you know what she's got away with her to read in there? In our lovely room which, pray God, we shall soon have back to ourselves? John Updike's *Couples*. Last night she was polishing off a Norman Mailer. What dark side of the Scots psyche is this I'm seeing?' she teased.

'She seems to be having a wonderful time,' said Abercrombie

uncomprehendingly. 'I would have taken a bet on it being a total disaster.' He leaned over and kissed Lulu satisfactorily on the lips. 'It's all down to you. You're a witch.'

They both went to see Abercrombie's aunt off at the station. She wanted to cry, she said, but didn't want to spoil the effect of her new hat. 'We'll see you soon,' Lulu promised. 'We'll be up in the summer.'

As she walked back down the platform with Abercrombie, Lulu said, 'Some day I might marry you, to please her. If you ask me.'

'I'm thinking about it,' he promised her. He looked em barrassed. 'You gave her such a good time. Can I say it? I'm so—grateful.'

'She needed taking out of herself. All that violence, all that repression.'

'You got her to confide in you. You're a very clever woman.'

Their arms entwined around each other's waists as they came out into the buffeting street wind. She was thinking of one parti-cular confidence. In the Tea Centre. When the aunt had said suddenly, 'It's a different world we live in nowadays. In my days, if a woman had a bairn out of wedlock, she was branded as a scarlet woman. Nowadays, all the thinking has changed.' Her hand holding the teacup had trembled, ever so slightly as she'd appealed to Lulu. 'Hasn't it?'

'Yes,' Lulu had responded. 'Nowadays, people are open.' And after that they'd gone and bought that hat.

DOUGLAS DUNN

Nymphs and Shepherds

Her professor liked her poems. They were as good as she was.
There was something decidedly virtuous in them. A sweetly-
complicated set of very nice hang-ups was unfolded in bold but
careful backhand on lined notepaper. All of a sudden the professor knew that this girl and her poems were what his professor-
ship and his vocation were all about. With a few more minutes,
his big harmless professorial mind had turned his rash guess that
it was also what life was about into a conviction as sound as that
the true hero of *Paradise Lost* is really the Devil.

Once or twice, as he was reading her poems quietly to himself,
he stopped to say, with his eyes still on the sheet of paper before
him, 'These are really quite good. Good. They're really . . . quite,
quite perfectly delightful poems.'

She already knew her poems were delightful, and got a bit
browned off with the professor, who by now had relaxed to a
point where he felt free to put his feet on his desk. 'I'm sick of
Old English riddles,' she confessed, breaking the mood with a
sigh. 'I'm fed up with Anglo-Saxon cross-gartered oafs belting
each other with battleaxes. I want to give it all up. What am I to
do?' It was a cry from the heart. It was a cry from the heart of a
beautiful and sensitive and highly intelligent girl post-graduate
student.

What she said troubled the professor, who did not take kindly
to the prospect of her saying farewell to his department. He

frowned understandingly and then went on reading. He was a bit sick of the Anglo-Saxons himself. Or he appeared to be reading. In fact, he was imagining a university of a sort he hoped that someone, one day, would give him carte blanche and allow him to devise. It was to be set in a park. Its small, discreet faculty buildings among the trees would look like a compromise worked by a Hobbit architect and the modern world. Lectures resembled picnics and tutorials resembled love affairs more than they did an imparting of knowledge. There, the professor dreamed, beautiful girl post-graduate students would not bother themselves with riddles composed in the devious minds of shamanistic Anglo-Saxon tricksters. They would write poems in bold but careful backhand on lined notepaper. They would sit under the elms reading Shakespeare and Keats. And as he looked at his student he decided that, well, no, perhaps she wasn't suited for that either. '*You* should be a shepherdess,' he said, pulling his feet off his desk in his excitement. 'That's it, that's undoubtedly it—a *shepherdess.*'

She scoffed at his ridiculous idea. But the professor went on and on about it until the thought of the wind on her cheeks and the lambs gambolling around her on the hillside took a hold on her imagination, too. In no time at all she had become as enthusiastic as he was for her pastoral future. At the same time she was well enough boned up on middle-aged professors to know that somehow, he was in this picture, this idyll, this highly alluring impossibility he was putting into her mind. 'If only,' she thought, '. . . if only.'

And then there was a moment of hallucinatory tenderness. All that beating about the bush the professor had started now stopped with a lulled, eye-opening decisiveness. 'You look like someone right now who wants to be a *shepherd*,' she said softly. When shy people like the girl post-graduate student announce, even in their round-about ways, to which they are prone, that they share your desire—well, the effect is devastating. There is no pulling back from *that* kind of proposition.

It *was* devastating. The professor sat back in his chair and thought he might have gone too far. 'Hello there,' he said to himself, 'now you've done it. You've gone completely over the score this time, you wicked old bachelor. Yes, you have.'

'No,' he said. 'I'd like to be a lamb—*your* lamb. I'd like to be your pet. That would be good enough for me. You see, I'm probably just that little bit too old for you.'

Strange and satisfactory things began to happen in the following few minutes. Suddenly the world seemed to improve. The professor's office felt alive with unnerving but soothing sensations. It was as if their gods kissed them each on the forehead. His would be an Anglo-Saxon King with horns in his helmet, an axe in one hand and an illuminated manuscript in the other, and with the stink of ale on his breath. Hers would be a shepherdess who looked invented by Fragonard in a fit of winsomely bucolic genius. They'd taken a shine to these two shy creatures; and, if it would make them happy . . .

In any case it all, as they say, happened. They were a happy couple. She walked the hills in her long shepherdess dress, in her pink hose, her shepherdess bonnet, in white shoes that had silver buckles, and with her shepherdess crook with ribbons tied to it and a pretty little golden bell that tinkled and amused the lamb that was always bounding along by her feet. When they stopped for a rest, she would read her latest poems to the lamb, who sat pampered and utterly spoiled on her lap, looking up at her with happy lamb eyes.

Other lambs in the flock were not jealous of this special creature that lived in the shepherdess house at the foot of the hill. It was deeply appreciated by the whole flock that one of their kind had at last avoided the inevitable. He, at least, would not end up in a mutton pie or a plate of Irish stew, and no one would pull him on in the form of a pure wool sweater when the cold snap came. They were glad for him.

Not a single cloud crossed the surface of their happy world until one day a truck arrived from the abattoir. The shepherdess

locked her lamb in the house, and, unable to face the sight of
her flock as they were herded away to their unfortunate destiny,
she set herself to performing a necessary task well away from that
tragic scene. But her lamb was an impertinent little devil. He was
the very caricature of his frisky species, and he managed to get
out of the house. Unable to tell the difference between him and
other lambs, the men rounded him up and bundled him into the
truck. Indignation and disappointment were bleated and baahed
by the entire flock; but the people who can be least expected to
understand sheep are the employees of an abattoir.

The shepherdess wept for days on end. She locked herself in
her house at the foot of the hill and wept.

Two or three weeks later she managed to pull herself together.
'A lamb, after all,' she reasoned, 'is a lamb; and a lamb cannot be
a professor, while a professor in turn cannot be a lamb, and I
must have been dreaming if I thought it had ever been possible.'
Yet she knew it had happened. Still, she had her whole life before
her. 'All that's necessary now,' she convinced herself, 'is a little
self-deception. It will be my secret.'

She undressed herself of her ridiculous outfit and got into the
T-shirt and jeans she'd been wearing that day when it all began in
the professor's study. Then she locked up her little house at the
foot of the hill and walked away from it. By the late evening, her
journey had involved several buses and two trains and she was in
some town or other in the Midlands. Within a month she met a
successful salesman in crockery. A month later they were married.

After a time, this hard-working and conscientious man realised
something was missing from the menu. One morning, on his
way out, in his suit, with his briefcase, he asked his wife, 'Any
chance of some lamb chops for tonight's dinner?' Her eyes closed
at the very thought of it. 'I'm . . . I'm allergic to it,' she said.

The poor fellow was extremely fond of lamb chops. Any kind
of lamb or mutton was very much to his taste. His mouth
watered at the idea of a nice lamb chop, or roast lamb, or kebabs.
So he asked her again. 'The smell, the touch, the taste, just any-

thing at all about lamb really turns me *off* !' she yelled.

Thinking this was extremely strange, and their marriage not going too well in any case, he bought a couple of lamb chops for himself. That sizzling frying sound, and a meaty aroma, drew her away from the television set. She broke down completely when she caught him red-handed in the kitchen preparing his lamb chops. Indeed, she was quite hysterical, and did uncharacteristic things like throw plates around. His challenging little supper had been meant to spite her; but the results were far more distressing than he'd bargained for, and he was sincerely apologetic. He grovelled. He offered to take her out for the evening. All she could say—shout, rather—was *'Sorry? Sorry?'* In the end she had to tell him the whole story. He thought she was mad. How could a professor turn into a lamb? Crockery salesmen, of course, cannot be expected to be particularly imaginative.

Weeks passed in an atmosphere of domestic contentions that was so thick you could have used it as olive oil. The more they talked about it, the more her husband began to think it wasn't all nonsense. So he began sneering at her, *'Lamb chops! Lamb chops!'* 'Another man, or men, in the past, well that,' he thought, 'is something I can live with. I've been no angel myself. It can only be expected of a woman as attractive as my wife. But a sheep! Sweet Jesus, that's too much!'

She left him. In fact they left each other, colliding with their suitcases in the hall as they issued frantically from their separate bedrooms. She went back to the university and buckled down to finishing her thesis on Anglo-Saxon riddles, spells and incantations, with special reference to Druidical magic, inasmuch as anything is known of it. Her divorce came through.

What she did not, could not know about, was that her lamb had survived. A professorial intelligence allied to a lamb's briskness of spirit, had encouraged him to make a break for it from the pen where the flock was spending its miserable last moments, waiting on the butchers returning from their tea-break. Melancholy sheep bleated a sad farewell as best they could in the circumstances, while the lamb stopped and turned, deeply moved by their good wishes, and in return offered them his thanks and sorrow with a choked baah.

For days he kept a low profile in suburban gardens. At night he sneaked along the grass verges of the roadside. It took him ages to get back to the little house at the foot of the hill. His exhilaration was dashed when he found it locked and deserted. At that moment he wanted nothing else than to lie down and die. But when he woke up, he wasn't a lamb, he was a professor again.

In the next months he searched high and low for the girl who had been his shepherdess. Anyone who saw that sorry sight of a man, in the streets of whatever town he was searching through, felt an instant compassion for his grievously red eyes, his down-at-heel shoes, his tousled hair and ragged clothes and his expression fixed in a manic resignation of shame and hopelessness. Then he, too, managed to get it together. He sat down by a roadside and sorted himself out as best he could.

It was therefore a shuddering surprise for everyone when he returned to his old campus looking for his job back. 'Where have you been?' It was a question for which he had nothing but contempt. But when he saw his girl post-graduate student walking across the campus square with books under one arm, and flicking her cigarette ash in a large concrete plant-pot, he broke down in an uncontrollable bleating. He steadied himself on the windowsill. It took him a full hour to reassemble his nervous system. He plucked madly on his jacket and sweater. But that insane sensation of his skin breaking into wool finally passed.

Then, bracing himself manfully into a fit of decision, he ran along several corridors, up and down several flights of stairs, over several quadrangles, until he reached the door of the girl post-graduates' common-room. Inside, young ladies were being young ladies together around a tea-machine, ruffling through women's magazines or looking at their faces in small hand-mirrors. He threw the door open with a resounding shove and a dozen girls looked round. 'No more platonic relationships!' he proclaimed

in a deep-chested bellow. Before they could laugh, one of them,
a girl who had been sitting alone in a corner, was running towards
the professor's outstretched arms.

ALAN SILLITOE

Confrontation

'When I saw you a year ago,' Mavis said resentfully, 'you told me you had only three months to live.'

He remembered it vividly—at June and Adrian's party. It was a disaster that was difficult to forget. What's more, his ploy hadn't worked, so he might just as well have saved himself the trouble of lying. Yet it *was* undeniable that he had lied. He could only apologise to her—first, because he was still here on earth to make her remind him of it; and second, that he was still alive and might yet lie again.

His apology didn't seem to make much difference. She watched him take a cigarette out of his packet, then put it back. He wasn't going to lie again, after all. Or perhaps it only meant that he wasn't going to smoke much today. He was showing her that he was cutting down his smoke production, so that at least he couldn't convincingly repeat his lie of a year ago.

'I've only got three months to live,' he had said.

She laughed, loud. 'You're joking.'

The folds of her red-and-white African safari wrap shifted under her laughter. She was big and fair and, talking to someone a few minutes ago, he'd heard that she had just left her husband. He thought he couldn't go wrong, until he told his stupid lie.

'Well, no, I'm not lying, or joking, though it sounds stupid, I admit. It was only this afternoon that I was told.' He looked straight into her face, and watched the expression change. If you weren't merciless to people who made fools of themselves they would never believe in you again.

Her features showed an inner terror, as if she had touched previously unfathomed depths of callousness in herself, and that this frightened her far more than any predicament he might be in at having only three months left to live.

'I'm sorry,' he said, 'really I am. I shouldn't have told you. You're the first one. Even my wife doesn't know. I only heard today, and I haven't been home yet. I went to see a blue movie in Soho, then came straight on to June and Adrian's.'

They stood in the small garden. Only a few people had sought refuge from the crushing noise because they thought it was still too damp outside. 'Are you here because you know June—or Adrian?' he asked.

It was his faint northern accent that brought back the feeling that he might still be lying. The only thing that stopped her disbelief was the fact that no one in the world would lie about such a matter. 'Both,' she told him.

'I don't even believe it myself,' he said, 'so if you think I'm lying I can easily understand it.'

Maybe so few people came into the garden, he thought, because it was close to the main road and a huge bar of orange sodium light glowing above the hedge had the ability to plunge its searching fire into any heart, and detect those untruths which everyone used at times like these. But against a monstrous lie it had no power.

She felt herself unfairly singled out to receive this terrible information about him. It was as if someone had come up and married her without her permission. Her soul had been sold in some under-the-counter slave-market. At the same time she felt privileged to be the first one told about it—though a gnawing uncertainty remained.

'Forget it,' he said. 'I shouldn't have spoken. I feel slightly ridiculous.'

Her husband had never told her anything. If he'd heard from his doctor that he was going to die he'd have kept the information to himself and slipped out of the world without a murmur. Her frequent and fervent cry had been: 'Why don't you *say* something? Speak!' Once when they got into bed, after a day of few words passing between them, she said in a friendly tone: 'Tell me a story, Ben!' He didn't even say good-night by way of reply. Thank God *that* was finished.

She touched his wrist. 'It's all right. It's better to speak.' The glass she held was empty. In the glow of the sodium light it was difficult to tell whether he was pale or not. Everyone looked ghastly under it, and she understood why most of the others stayed inside. Adrian and June must have bought the house in the summer, when the days were long.

'It's not,' he said, 'but I'm one of those people who can't help myself. If I'm not talking I'm not alive. I often wonder if I talk in my sleep.'

Illness that is fatal, she had read, was nearly always brought on because the inner spirit of the afflicted person was being prevented from opening and flowering—or simply from a lack of the ability to talk about yourself and your problems. He didn't seem to be stricken in that way at all, though every rule must have its exception, as they say.

'I've often thought of buying one of those ultra-sensitive modern Japanese tape-recorders which are switched on by the sound of your own voice,' he said, 'then playing it back in the morning to see if I've uttered either any profundities, banalities, or just plain baby-talk during the night.'

Her husband, who had been in advertising, had believed so much in the power of the spoken word that he would say very little, except perhaps at work, where it could be taken down and transcribed by his secretary, and used to make money. She dredged around at the back of her mind for something to say. Maybe her husband had been right when, in reply to one of her stinging accusations that he never said anything, he said: 'It takes two to make a silence.'

'But I never did,' he laughed. 'They're too expensive. Anyway, I might say something that would frighten me to death! And when I say something, I like to make up my mind about what I'm going to say a second or two beforehand.'

'Is that what you're doing now?'

People were coming out through the open French windows with plates of food. Neither the sodium lights, nor the damp, would bother them if they had something to do, such as eat.

'Absolutely,' he told her, 'but because I'm talking to *you* I don't let it stop me.'

The northern accent, slight as it was, far from making him seem untrustworthy, now had something comforting about it. If he'd had the accent, and spoken very little, it would have been merely comic. But he had something to say, and that was different. He was also using it to good effect.

'What work do you do?' It wasn't much to ask, but it was better than nothing.

He named one of the minor publishing houses that employed him. 'But I'll be giving that up—*force majeur.*'

'Perhaps things aren't as bad as you think.'

He suddenly got tired of it, and thought that if he didn't go and talk to somebody else he really would be dead in three months—or even three minutes—from boredom. 'I must have a drink,' he said. 'Be back soon.'

Later she saw him from a distance, talking intently to someone else. He came behind her in the queue for food, turned round because he'd forgotten to pick up his napkin-roll of knife-and-fork, and looked at her as if she were a mirror. Thank God she'd stopped herself in time from smiling and saying something. After heaping up his plate with a choice of everything he walked over and talked to a woman with grey hair, an iron face, and a big bust.

She observed him for a while, convinced he wasn't spinning the same tragic tale he'd put out to her—though not doubting that it was something with an equal bite. He wore a formal and finely-cut navy-blue suit, had black hair and dark eyes, which did make him look even more pallid under the light inside the house.

She asked someone who he was, and they said: 'Oh, that's Tom Barmen'—so she went upstairs to where June and Adrian kep the telephone, and the directories, and found that he lived in Muswell, which wasn't far away. She dialled the number, and a woman's voice answered.

'Would you rather be a man or a woman?' Joy Edwards asked, when Mavis got to the bottom of the stairs.

'Depends for how long,' she said.

'All day,' Harry Silk laughed, muscles bulging under his sweat-shirt, a hand flattened on his bald head.

'Five minutes,' said his wife, heavily pregnant.

This was more like a party, Mavis thought, saying: 'Both at once? Or one at a time?' and went to the bar for another glass of white wine, not caring now whether she got tight or not. She'd said all she had to say, for one evening at least.

When the doorbell rang, sounding faintly above the noise, she thought it was a taxi come to collect someone. Because it was after midnight, one or two people had already left. A tall woman, still with her coat on, pushed through the crowd. By the kitchen door there was a crash of (unfilled) coffee cups, though the woman who had just arrived was not the cause.

'It's Phillis Barmen,' she heard someone say.

She met him a year later at a publisher's cocktail party in the huge new Douglas Hotel. In the crowd she saw a hand throw down the end of a cigarette so that it went into a tray of peanuts instead of the ashtray. She looked up and saw who it was. He was dressed in the same suit—or one very similar.

'Did I?' he said, in response to her accusation. 'I'm sorry about that. Parties are so deadly bloody boring.'

'The end of the last one, where we met, was quite exciting—I thought,' she reminded him.

'Thanks to you.' He looked as if he wished that *she* had only three months to live—or less.

'I suppose we should both apologise.'

She was totally miscast in her assumptions, he said to himself. Her mind was misshapen, the whole bloody lot warped.

She sensed she was mis-reading everything, judging from his mischievous look. It was devilish.

'You were chosen,' he said. 'I knew I could rely on you, though you were so long going to the telephone that I was beginning to wonder whether I'd made a mistake. But when I saw you go up the stairs I knew I'd picked a winner.'

He had taken her seriously, at least.

She had taken *him* seriously, which wasn't bad going.

'I needed one more public shindig with my wife to end my deadly boring marriage,' he said. 'She wanted it too, so never feel guilty. It was quite mutual. We're well shut of each other now. I did feel sorry for June and Adrian, though.'

'So did I.'

'But they couldn't say they were bored for that last half-hour.'

She couldn't resist gloating: 'All this is pure hindsight on your part.'

'There's no such thing as hindsight, in my way of looking at things.'

'You didn't plan it at all,' she persisted.

She felt so kicked in the stomach that when he asked her to go out to dinner after the party she said yes, and from that time on never had a moment to wonder whether she'd done the right thing or not. It became more and more obvious however that she'd been just as scheming when she'd gone upstairs to make the telephone call at June and Adrian's party, and over the years it was easy enough to make sure that he knew it.

B. A. YOUNG

Symbiosis

They sat in the hide together for an hour waiting for a shot. The hide was built of brushwood and covered in canvas and corrugated iron to blend with the country. You kept your head below the corrugated iron, but you could see, through the little slits at eye-level, a rolling landscape of short green vegetation with some taller growth that Raymond called 'trees'. On the right was a small group of buildings. It was a good hide. Raymond made it early in the morning, before the light came, and they moved into it before dawn to get the horse on their first run.

When the light showed, Raymond said the horse would come out from behind the *farm* and cross from left to right quite slowly, and they could get a shot in before the earthies began their day's work and dispersed them. Raymond was an earthie from the local tribe. Zat was often angry at his parade of regional knowledge, but it could be useful.

Zat turned off the switch on the firing-circuit of his projector and blew some dust from the transparent cover of the laser-light. There seemed to be no dust in the air, which was cool and still, the leaves motionless on the *trees*, a trail of smoke from the building rising vertically into the air, but somehow some dust had settled on the sight. It was going to be a bad day.

'You think the horse will come?' he asked.

'They come every day.'

'They haven't come today.'

'Sometimes they don't come.'

'You said they come every day.'

'Usually they do.'

'I wish I could speak your language better.'

From the yard at the back of the *farm* a small tractor made a coughing sound and began to move into the open. It looked like a red beetle on the vivid green of the ground vegetation. It crept slowly across in front of the hide, taking the exact path Raymond had said the horse would take when they came down to graze. Zat lowered his projector to his knee.

'That's it then. They won't come now.'

'Wait a while,' Raymond said. 'Tractors won't spook a horse. A railway-train will spook them, or one of your saucers. Not a tractor.'

'There aren't any horse anyway.'

Two horse came from behind the buildings, one behind the other. They were both chestnuts, the front one very big, the second not so big but big enough. They moved slowly away from the *farm* in the wake of the tractor. Zat activated his circuit and took a sample sighting with his projector.

'Not yet,' Raymond said. 'They will come across the front and you will get a better shot.'

For horse you want to get a charge through the shoulder into the heart. The skull is very thick and a hand projector will only penetrate it at one or two points, but a charge will go through the shoulder or the chest and paralyse the action of the heart. Zat was angry that Raymond should tell him what to do, but he knew he was right and he took his advice though pretending that he did it on his own initiative.

The two horse moved diagonally towards the hide. The ground sloped quite sharply down into a small valley with a thin growth of dark green vegetation lining the course of the lowest contour and then sloped up again towards the hide. Behind the horse the ground rose to a crest that made a curve against the blue, lightly-clouded sky like the stomach of a pregnant woman. Zat took a fresh sight on the leading horse. The muscles of his belly tensed and he held his breath as he aligned the sight on the animal.

Over the crest a small saucer sailed, barely high enough to clear the scattered *trees*, its motors screaming from their worn bearings, its paintwork red with rust and black with oil-streaks where seals no longer fitted. It was flying very slowly towards the hide, losing height gradually until when it was over the bottom of the valley you could look down on it. The bigger of the two horse threw up its head with a snort and galloped back to where it had come from. The other followed it.

Zat cut off his firing-circuit and lowered the butt of his projector to the ground. 'That's it then,' he said.

'They won't come out with that,' Raymond said.

'The bastard.' Zat came out from the hide, waving an arm at the saucer in a threatening movement. The saucer landed lower down the side of the valley and a figure emerged, tall and thin and standing with a forward curve in the backbone. Zat recognised him as a road engineer called Tarkas.

'Wait here,' he said. He walked downhill towards the saucer until he was within earshot. 'Are you in trouble?'

'There is always trouble with these things,' Tarkas said.

'But specifically? You barely cleared the hill.'

'Specifically yes. I am only getting forty per cent output from the generator. But this is a good place. I am quite pleased to be here.'

'You have spoilt my day,' Zat told him.

'It's a beautiful day. How have I spoilt it? The temperature is right, the humidity is right, there is no industrial development except there in the valley.'

'I came to shoot horse.'

'That is foolish. Why do you not get your servant to shoot a horse for you?'

'I shoot for pleasure. It reassures me that my physical reactions are in good condition.'

'What will you do with your horse when you have shot it?'

'What do you do with anything when you have shot it?'

'I try not to shoot anything unless it threatens me.'

'I see we don't talk the same language.'

'There is some earthie beer in the saucer,' Tarkas said. They went together to the saucer. Tarkas's earthie servant Dennis brought a folding table and two chairs from the saucer and pitched them on the grass. While they drank the beer, Dennis cooked some bird's eggs. Zat called Raymond from the hide and sent him to eat with Dennis.

'I should have introduced myself,' he said. 'My name is Zat. I'm the Commissioner at Stow-on-the-Wold.'

'I knew you already,' Tarkas said. 'I have read your account of your first landing on this planet and the fighting after. That was good. That was poetic. That wasn't shooting horse.'

'I haven't shot one yet.'

'You will. What else have you shot? The fauna of this planet is being decimated.'

'It's part of my business to ensure that it is kept at the proper level.' Zat was angry but he wanted to hear what the engineer had to say. It was becoming common for the settlers to take the earthie side nowadays, he thought. 'I bagged a fine bull ox last week near Sezincote. Although I am responsible for giving permits to shoot game, I only gave myself a permit for one bull. Does that sound better?'

'And the bull? What did you do with that?'

'I shall have the head mounted and hung in the Residency. The rest we gave to the earthies. They eat them.'

'Exactly. Also they eat sheep. Will you shoot sheep?'

'I am not hunting sheep now, but yes, when I have a good horse I shall go after a sheep.'

'How many sheep will you allow yourself?'

'Why do you ask these questions?'

'I am interested in the native way of life. They have a symbiotic life with the local fauna, the sheep, the oxen, even I think the horse. We are disturbing the ecology.'

'My experts tell me not.'

Tarkas sighed and drank the beer remaining in the bottom of his mug. 'I have to look at a road bridge at Cheltenham,' he said. 'Does your servant know about generators?'

'A little.' Zat called Raymond and Tarkas explained what had to be done. Raymond fixed the generator in five minutes and Tarkas gave him a five-credit piece.

'Will it fly me to Cheltenham?'

'Driven carefully.'

Zat said, 'You're not in a hurry, are you?'

'Not specially.'

'I would like to talk to you about the symbiotic life of the earthies and the other fauna. I find this very interesting. Sometimes I get the idea that the the men call the other beasts by name and get them to perform simple tricks.'

'A good idea. This is what happens.'

'I know about the milk from the oxen and the wood from the sheep. You think the animals cooperate in this?'

'It is a symbiotic existence,' Tarkas said. 'The oxen need to be relieved of their milk because if they are not it causes them pain. So they have trained the men to take it. As for the sheep, when their hair is too long for comfort, at the start of the hot season, they get the men to cut it short for them. The men use the waste to make fabrics. I expect this is what your servant is wearing.'

Zat called Raymond over and caught hold of a loose panel of his clothing. 'What is this made from, Raymond?'

'Terylene.'

'Do you get this from the waste hair of the sheep?'

'They make it in a factory.'

'Yes, but is it from sheep-hair? Wood?'

'Wool,' Raymond corrected him. 'Wool is only for the upper classes. Terylene is a long-chain synthetic polyamide resin. It is produced by the reaction between polybasic acids and polyfunctional amines. It is what you would call one of our folk industries.'

'That is a clever man,' Tarkas said to Zat.

He took off for Cheltenham soon after. The sun was high now, the shadows shortening on the ground. There was a lot of game about, a herd of cow on the far side of the valley, a knot of perhaps thirty sheep grazing further away to the left. Zat sent Raymond to the land-car to bring his files; he would do some work until later when the temperature became lower. He opened a file about a *strike* of the earthie workers at a *brewery* at Donnington and dozed off into a light sleep.

He slept for about an hour. When he woke up two earthies were standing in front of him. They were only part-grown, the bigger one about four and a half feet, the other perhaps half a foot less. The smaller one had a length of ox-skin strap in his hand. This one kept repeating some words in the local dialect. Zat tried to understand but it meant nothing to him.

'Sina domista?'

Zat said, 'Speak more slowly.'

'Sina domista?' the boy repeated.

'Slowly. Slow-ly.'

'Sina domista avya?'

Zat was ridiculously embarrassed. He tried repeating the words back as he heard them. 'Seena dawmista?'

'Avya?'

A small animal, reddish-brown, ran round the side of the wood, a dog, but not worth a shot. The dog ran quite fast to the smaller boy and the boy leaned down and fastened the end of his thong into a ring attached to a collar that went round the dog's neck. The dog stood quite still while this was happening, panting slightly but not at all scared of the boy. Zat wondered if there was a symbiotic relationship between them. He made a sentence of words he knew in the dialect.

'You-yourself and dog friends?'

The boy said nothing but stretched his mouth into a smile. The bigger boy said something that sounded like 'Cmon' and the two of them ran down towards the *farm*. The dog went with them, trying to run faster than the boys but restrained by the leather strap. I should have kept them here, Zat thought, I should have asked about the symbiotic relationship between the boy and the dog. It is a matter of some importance possibly. He turned back to his file and was asleep against almost at once.

Raymond woke him. 'Dinner in ten minutes?'

'All right.'

Zat felt fresher after his sleep. He read through the rest of his file, making notes in the margins, while Raymond put a table in front of him with a native plate on it. When Raymond brought the pot with the *stew* he had made, Zat told him to fetch another chair. 'Bring another plate. I want to talk.'

While they ate, Raymond explained about the boy and the dog. It was simple, he said; the boy was fond of the dog and the dog was fond of the boy.

'You mean they both feel the same emotions?'

'Why not?'

'They are not the same species.'

'We are not the same species. They have lived together a long time. They have an understanding. Also sympathy.'

'You mean they have a symbiotic relationship?' Zat asked.

'I don't know what a symbiotic relationship is.'

'The dog needs the man, the man needs the dog.'

'You could say that.'

'Fetch some more beer from the land-car,' Zat said. 'Bring one for yourself. You like beer?'

'I have a symbiotic relationship with beer.'

Raymond came back with a *sixpack* and opened two tins. 'Listen,' Zat said, 'I want to get this clear. The emotion the dog has for the boy is the same as the emotion the boy has for the dog. The boy and the dog are equals.'

'In a way.'

'One isn't more important than the other.'

'They both have their functions.'

'And this is the same with, say, the sheep?'

'The sheep have their own functions.' Raymond began to explain what they were, but Zat realised that what he was saying was what Tarkas had said a while back.

'I want to go down the hill to see the *farm*,' he said.

Raymond took the plates and the unopened beer back to the land-car and they went together down the hill, the trees speckled where the sun made dark shadows under the leaves, the crest of the hill across the valley rising higher into the sky as they descended. Three sheep looked at them curiously, but Raymond threw a stone at them and they ran away. At the outskirts of the *farmyard* the taller of the two boys was sitting on a gate made from bent steel tubes. Raymond said something to him in Inglish and he climbed down and went into the house.

They waited outside the gate and a man came to them from inside the house. He was tall for an earthie, and wore the dark trappings common to the richer men, three garments that covered all the limbs, with a white *shirt* underneath bound at the throat with a narrow strip of coloured material. 'Ask him if he speaks our language,' Zat said.

Raymond asked him. 'He says he speaks a few words,' he reported.

'This is what I want to know,' Zat said to the *farm* man. 'Do you have a symbiotic relationship with the domestic fauna?' The farm man looked at him, his mouth open, his eyes uncomprehending. 'Ask him in Inglish,' Zat told Raymond.

'I don't think there is an Inglish word for "symbiotic relationship".'

'Ask if he can call the fauna by their names and they will come to him.' Raymond translated this to the man and the man gave a sharp cry, 'Ereboi!' and the dog came and stood by him.

'And the oxen?'

'This will be harder.' The man led them through the gate where the boy had been sitting. There was a female ox about fifty yards away, facing them, its head held low so that it could eat the fresh shoots of the ground plants. The farm man made a sound like 'Daisy' and the ox stopped eating and began to walk towards them. When it was a dozen paces away it halted as if uncertain what to do, and made a low monosyllabic sound.

They spent an hour at the *farm*. The man showed them how to call the oxen and the sheep, and also how the dog could call the sheep. The dog could not call the oxen, nor the oxen the sheep, but the man had control of all three, and the dog and the oxen could communicate with the man, though only in a limited way. Zat gave the *farm* man a five-credit piece and the man spat some saliva to the ground and gave the money back to him. 'This is a gesture of friendship,' Raymond explained hastily.

The sun was beginning to decline and there would not be much more light. Zat suggested that instead of going back to the hide they should go to the other side of the hill and see if there were any horse at the back of the *farm* buildings. Zat walked ahead up the slope, not wanting to talk, wanting to think about what he had learnt during the day, the symbiotic relationships between the earthies and the other animals, the earthies more intelligent but animals themselves, in spite of their galaxoid shape, part of a pattern of existence he had not fully understood before. He could hear Raymond behind him, his ox-skin shoes rustling in the fallen leaves. They went through the wood and came out at a point where the sun was directly in front of them and it was difficult at first to see down into the valley.

Raymond came and stood beside him. 'Horse!' he said softly. 'Do you see? Near the big tree.'

There were two horse grazing in front of a big, irregularly shaped tree with red-brown leaves, their heads down at ground level, their long, dark-coloured tails flicking lazily to brush the flies off their flanks. They were the same two they had seen in the morning. Zat told Raymond to go down the hill and drive them towards the farm buildings and Raymond moved off, quietly, with the expression he often wore, half excitement, half contempt. Zat activated his firing circuit and sighted his projector on the point where the horse would pass on their way to the *farm*. The horse were taking no notice of Raymond, who was shouting at them and making a movement with his arms.

Zat decided he would risk a shot at the larger horse where it was by the tree. Horse were not exciting, he would polish off the single horse he had allowed himself on his licence and try something better. He fixed his laser-spot on the shoulder at the base of the neck, but something moved over to the left, a better target, sharp against the *grass* in the afternoon sun, moving at a sharp clip towards the horse. Zat tensed himself inside, leaning on his breath, and held the spot on the new target, halfway up the breast where the shot would tell, a little below the armpit. The projector moved in a slow arc, keeping the spot on the vital point, then Zat, cool, confident, happy with the excitement of the shot, touched the switch and the target fell forward dead caught cleanly with the first charge, lying now face downwards in the *grass* and twitching slightly. Zat had been reluctant before about shooting man for sport, but after what he had learnt now, that man and the other game were equal factors in a complex pattern of which only the pattern itself mattered, there seemed no reason why it should not be included. True, he had not issued himself a licence, but he could do that when he got back to the land-car.

Another brace of man came out of the *farm* moving quickly over the *grass*, straight and graceful in the late sun. Zat took a sight on the leading one, the smaller of the two, the younger brother of the one he had bagged, but decided not to risk another shot until he had regularised the licence. As he had said to Tarkas, game must be hunted with proper restraint.

GILES GORDON

The Red-Headed Milkman

Edward's life was earthbound. He had been born neither angel nor fairy (assuming he believed in either), and he hadn't trained or been trained as an aviator. One day he was inspired to fly, to try to fly. His sense of well-being, of rightness with the world and with himself, was such that he believed he might be able to do so. He stood on the lawn at the back of his and Ann's house, wearing an open-necked shirt and shorts and plimsolls. Ann stood in the garden, watching him. She was wearing a loose summer dress, of swirling Monet-like blues and greens. Why she was standing there—not, for instance, sitting, or doing something of her own, or even gardening, and she was the gardener—was not revealed in the mind of either of them, or to the other. It was a hot, bright, sunny day. The dullness inside the house may have forced them into the light outside for the brighter the outside world, the greyer the inside seemed.

He jumped in the air, not rationalising the activity but believing, vaguely believing that he would rise beyond the height he had consciously jumped, the height he knew he could physically reach. What joy! He jumped in the air, knowing that he would rise up, soar, float, be at one with the elements rather than battling against them.

If, in advance of jumping, he had asked what chances she thought he had of reaching up there, touching the sky and cavorting about in the blue, she would have given him little encouragement.

She wouldn't necessarily have advised against the activity—after all, he was free agent, if he wanted to jump in the air that was his business, he should go ahead and do so—but in intellectual or in any other terms she would have given him not a flea's chance; which may have been why he didn't consult her before taking his feet off the ground; which in itself presupposes that he'd taken the decision to leap, so he could—theoretically and in principle— have discussed it with his wife.

He jumped in the air and she watched him do so. Whether she understood or realised that his aim and ambition was to reach further up than the two or three feet which in fact he reached was not revealed by him to her, by her to him. She was, in her mind, to herself, a sceptical onlooker but she loved Edward, she loved her husband Edward, and she would have believed in her heart that he could fly if it was important to him that he should. She wouldn't have conceded as much to him but that in no way invalidated her faith in his aspirations. Not that she believed that he would fly, but that he could. For man can do what man will do. The summer day, the browning of the skin, the birds, the song.

He jumped in the air, feet off the ground, both together, up. It was a hot August day. He wore shorts and an open-necked shirt. She wore a cotton dress, had bare legs and feet, her hair a-swept about. There was a ruffle of wind in the air, in the leaves of the trees, the heavy branches holding up their discreet greenery.

She thought: I love Edward. Dear Edward. My husband. And she thought of her love for him in a way different from her love for their children.

He was in the air, his feet off the ground, off the grass. Look: Edward is trying to fly.

She thought: He wants to fly. Is he less likely to do so with my believing in my heart of hearts (but not, admittedly, my mind of minds) that he has the potential, the capacity than if I thought, even said: How infantile? and wrinkled my nose. A man leaping off a faded, sun-burnt lawn into the blue air isn't going to fly, however exhilarated he may feel. Particularly when he's not a scientist, understands nothing—nothing—about science and technology. Can he mend a fuse? Does he comprehend electricity? Even how the telephone works, or a motor car? Levitation doesn't that way come, not in the lives of those who continue to be marginally sane.

She looked, was looking, and he jumped. Bravo, she thought, and she encouraged him (why shouldn't she, if that was what he wanted to do: human beings need encouragement in almost any circumstances), saying:

'Go on, Edward, jump.'

He was too determined, concentrating on what he was doing, the strenuous and complex activity of jumping, to be able to look at his wife at that moment and smile, acknowledge her encouragement, her commitment to his action. But her encouragement meant much to him. Would it be too much to say that it meant everything to him, whether or not she recognised as much? Would that be an emotional, exaggerated statement merely? Her encouragement, her belief in him made it possible, in actuality, for him to believe that he could fly. Indeed, without her silent, undisclosed support he couldn't, wouldn't have contemplated the idea of flying. Which was why he hadn't specifically asked her for her blessing, for if she had denied him her belief, and he had assumed (wrongly) that she would have done, he would have been thrown into depression, humiliation, defeat. Flying, after all, wasn't something he did often. It wasn't something he'd achieved before. He was neither Daedalus nor Icarus, though decades ago he had liked to imagine himself as the former, probably because from an early age—certainly by his late teens— he realised he would never be an especially practical person. Indeed, he continued to marvel each night that he'd somehow got through the live-long day. 365 times a year, too. Leap year was another thing he'd never quite understood.

He jumped. Into the air. Up. An upward motion. He did so only because he was exhilarated, stimulated by being alive, for having shared a life, shared lives for so many years with Ann, and with their miraculous, maddening children. (Quite how *they'd* appeared on the scene was something else he was a bit bemused by.) It was a day in which—and for which—to jump for joy, simple, uncomplicated joy, and he felt inclined to do so, and because he loved his wife, naked and clothed, and because he loved his wife and she was there, present, in the summer garden with him, that he was with her, their lives were together at that time, parallel, converging lines, vanishing points ceasing to vanish at a particular point, at one. Not forgetting the children, the children, he could hear the children, and the intensity of the jump, the aspiring, leaping ambition. The moment had passed, no, not passed, changed, shifted, become diluted like lime juice cordial doused with water. And because of the sun, the heat, the haze, the mind had gone. And the voices of the children passed as anything passes, as trebles broke and gave way to growls in the throat, gruff in the mouth, tears in the mind.

Edward failed to fly, failed to jump in the air. At his age he wouldn't do anything so silly, would he? A father proceeding through his third decade, an unprofessional man holding down a responsible job. That was, he kept a secretary behind a typewriter. And there was laughter in the garden—fresh not furtive laughter, strawberries and cream, sunshine laughter; not complex, devious, ebony laughter reflected off itself—and his face was thrown back and up and so was hers, their two faces shining and up, touched by the sun and drinking it, and their heads were all over the place, roaring at the blue day, their faces everywhere but in the orbit of each other, shaking like mops out of a third floor window, and they were, pause, a heart beat, pause, happy. Edward. Ann. Smiles and smiles of a golden, city afternoon. Cities comprise large numbers of people grouped together in houses on relatively small areas of land. The buildings tend to rise up as much as they spread out, increasingly so too.

That is, was: the pain of getting through life, of everyday living, was numbed momentarily, isolated for a time by lightness and laughter, a sweet cocaine.

Suddenly—oh suddenly—the laughter wrenched shut in his throat, was stifled, sawn off, and he said, he said, shading his voice:

'Are you happy?'

and her laughter, her abandoned serenity, her at-oneness-with-the-world ceased, and he said:

'Are you happy?'

and she looked solemn and afraid, as if a cloud had been cast, and she said:

'Happy?'

She was repeating what he had said, parroting him, for want of time or space to say something other, to think about the reason for the question and at that time and what it might portend. For want of a nail, not to mention a horse. Lucky horse, unlucky nail.

He said: 'If I left you today?'

Where was the gaiety in that, that remark, a question, and the sky was still above them and the colour it usually was at that time of year and on such a bright and sunny day, and the leaves on the branches veiled the garden from the outside world and they nodded and bobbed and trembled, a little gust of wind, as reflecting the question, afraid of it.

'If I left you today?'

The first time, ever, he'd said it, and after so many years together; and his tone of voice added nothing to the words, conveyed not a clue to the intention. She had always—always, since first meeting him—thought it would come because it usually did, as it did, didn't it, with men and women, husbands and wives, people and people, but as long as the children were creating, being created, creating themselves she had harboured the hope that it would be put off, delayed, the departure held up. She had thought it would come, always, but had never feared it. The fear could come when it came, if it had to. Why anticipate a loss of light?

'If I left you today?'

Like a bubbling, crashing waterfall the implications pushed

upon her, and they weren't selfish, by no means not of the abandoned woman kind, the wronged wife, of what she would do now, how she would cope, as if it were a speculation rather than had been mentioned, asserted, the question posed. The future crowded in suddenly, welled in her skull, a concentration of years to come. She understood at once that he would very likely see more of the children, know them better as an absent father, taking them out for a weekend day, than he did living with them in the same house. At home he concentrated little upon them, gave up hardly any of his time to them and their affairs specifically. If it suited him, his inclinations, he'd do things with them. Was it because he was bored by the idea of football that they were, that he'd never taken them to a football match? Were they in that respect deprived children?

'If I left you today?'

There was always tomorrow, always tomorrow, but brother there wasn't, she thought, sister there wasn't. There was a sour, closed expression on her lips, a smear of wide sticky tape, gummed strip, brown, opaque not at all transparent, not Sellotape, the kind you have to lick, muzzling her mouth, forbidding a wasted or dead life to pour out. It was easy to despise those you loved. Those? she thought. Who are the others? And she only despised the question, his suggestion that he might flit.

You bastard, she thought. I still love you. How is it possible to stop loving? Not, she added as a corrective to her mind, that I think you're unworthy of my love. That's not it at all. That would be a flattering unction to myself, to my own peace of mind.

She looked up. There should have been clouds in the sky. There wasn't one.

He looked at her. Once he had loved her. That had to be reckoned with. Not just loved her but fallen sinker, line and hook in love with her, a meshing and gliding and spinning and abandon and gilding of lambs and moisture and lyricism and owls and full moons over new water and the twinkling, sparkling lights of piers and circuses and a continual squeezing of rich colour with fat and body in it from tubes of oil paint. O my love! O my memory!

He looked at her. Her arm, her head, the angle at which she held her chin, the spread fingers flickered, shot, defended she knew not what. They were raised to protect her face from she knew not what: the crackelure of the future, perhaps? Not her, please God, not her. Let her remain . . . and he knew that she wasn't as young as the shape she'd been the day before yesterday. She was older, yes, of course. But that was all, the only difference from what she had been. And she wanted to be old, to shudder onwards. She despised intimations of what hadn't been, of what she hadn't been. She was still the woman he'd loved, the woman he'd married. Had the mirage, if such it was, been her, or his love for her, or him, her love for him? And was it a mirage, was that a proper way to confront it? Had it ever been one, a glimpse in a mirror or a look at a painting long since altered or faded, losing its nature, its identity? Was it right to think of experience, of time passed and past as so much dross, something to be neglected or rejected in terms of the present?

Edward thought: What have I said? What has the sun done to me? I'm happy. Aren't I? And wondered where the measurement of happiness began.

Then he heard the shrill voices of the children again, coaxing themselves forward towards the very adulthood, the very maturity he was eschewing, denying, puzzling over. And yet, and yet, could the present, the future even, be based on, built on nostalgia? Could it be, let alone should it be?

She looked at him, Ann at her husband Edward, soberly, circumspectly: what was he on about? What was he? Then a wilder thought: Who was he?

She was appalled, shocked, depressed, wasn't she? That he had said what he had (his words had rung out:—If I left you today?) because, having said it, he hadn't presumably made up his mind to leave them, to leave her. If he had decided, he wouldn't, would he, have put the question but informed her that he was leaving, or kept the information to himself and gone. For God's sake go, she thought. For God's sake go, she wanted to say.

He saw her shaking her head at him, as if bewildered by his concern, his anxiety on her behalf. As if saying: What is it? And she held out her hand to him, the long arm reaching out and the palm at the end, the strong, assertive, work-worn fingers. Then the other hand, or was it only one, not to embrace but to encounter, to touch, even to prove that they existed, the pair of them, Edward and Ann, the one to the other, each to each. She said to him:

'You are happy, aren't you?'
knowing he was, knowing he was, being certain of that, his image in her head, winding and unwinding, the reel playing on the screen over and over again.

'You are happy, aren't you?'
she said to him, her voice aloud across the pocket handkerchief of lawn, because—she didn't add—you seem it, you're so much more relaxed these days, you take things as they come, as far as I know, as far as I can tell, as far as I can ever tell. And he wondered if he was retreating towards silence, towards the great unspoken divide. O God have mercy on our wrinkling, veined bodies after we have renewed the planet, as we continue to toil. O God have mercy on our living souls.

She, his wife, what of her? he wondered. She remained so inscrutable, so child-fulfilled that he couldn't know, or didn't know, what the raging enigma of her everyday sobriety portended. Could her soul be as serene as he had the impression it was, and why should that outrage his mind as much as did the fact that a minority of the population went to church and presumably derived more from the experience than they possessed scepticism to criticise it? You can't unpeel people, he thought. You can't even lay yourself open, spread yourself out and be certain that you've unravelled the mystery.

Her hand went out to him and he shook his head as he jumped, jumped, tried to ... fly? soar? escape? Her hand reached out towards him and he shook his head, denying the hand. Her hand reached to him and she brushed his waist, touched it, and he fell to the ground, collapsed in a crumpled heap, didn't move, was almost ostentatiously still.

'You're not hurt, are you?' she said, instantly afraid, a hammer on the anvil of her heart.

She saw a finger in the telephone dial, the penultimate hole, the dial whirring round three times, then the bell and blue light of an ambulance, and a wheelchair for life, for after life. And the apple blossom in the long Warwickshire garden with the cottage at one end, its whitewash dazzling in the sunshine, and the parched brown fields at the other circled by crows, endlessly arced by black birds. That was a memory of the passionate imagination, a romantic never-never land rather than an exact recalling of an episode in their young life together, though it was that too, Edward and Ann, new lovers. It was only years later that they seemed, in the memory, new then. At the time they'd thought of themselves as lovers since the world began, as if each of them knew everything there was to know about the other, and more than there was to know. Ann focused back to the present.

He was getting to his feet easily. There was nothing wrong with him, he'd fallen to the ground because he wanted to. He was hugging his body jealously, as if it was all in the world that remained to him.

'I don't know what I'm talking about,' he said. 'Of course I'm happy.'

She smiled at him, in her blue and green cotton dress, he in his shorts and open-necked shirt and plimsolls. She knew, accepted and understood, that she'd been secure all the time. all the time. Didn't she? She paused in her mind. Didn't she? The sun smiled down, the foliage rocked gently, a cradle indeed to the children within. Frailty, thy name is humanity.

He said, in a quiet still voice, 'I suppose I've always been frightened you might walk out.' And he hoped she didn't think he was worried about being left with the children, for that wasn't it at all, that had nothing to do with his concern.

'Me?' she said. And then, 'Honestly, is that what you think?'

He shrugged, pursed his lips.

She said, astonished, astonished, her whole body puffing up with amazement:

'Who with?'

He hadn't thought of her as leaving with anyone, anyone in particular. Just that she'd have had enough of him, had enough, gone. He said:

'Oh, I don't know. The red-headed milkman?'

And they both laughed.

'It's too hot to jump in the air,' said Edward. And Ann didn't disagree.

GRAHAM SWIFT

Gabor

'This is Gabor,' said my father in a solemn, rehearsed, slightly wavering voice.

This was early in 1957. The war was still then quite fresh in the memory—even of those, like myself, who were born after it. Most households seemed to have framed photographs of figures in uniform, younger Dads, jauntily posed astride gun barrels, sitting on wings. Across the asphalt playground of my County Primary School the tireless struggle between English and Germans was regularly enacted. This was the only war, and its mythology ousted other, lesser intrusions into peace. I was too young to be aware of Korea. Then there was Suez, and Hungary.

'Gabor, this is Mrs Everett,' continued my father, enunciating slowly, 'Roger's Mummy. And this is Roger.'

Gabor was a lanky, dark-haired boy. He was dressed in a worn black jacket, a navy blue jumper, grey shorts, long grey socks and black shoes. Only the jacket and limp haversack, which he held in one hand, looked as if they were his. He had a thick, pale, straight-sided face, dark, horizontal eyes and a heavy mouth. Above his upper lip—I found this remarkable because he was only my age—was a crescent of gossamer, blackish hairs, like a faint moustache.

'Hello,' said my mother. Poised in the doorway, a fixed smile on her face, she was not at all clear what was to be done on occasions like this—whether motherly hugs or formality were required. She had half expected to be ready with blankets and soup.

Father and the newcomer stood pathetically immobile on the doorstep.

'Hello Gabor,' I said. One adult custom which seemed to me, for once, eminently practical, and vindicated by moments like this, was to shake hands. I reached out and took the visitor's wrist. Gabor went a salmony colour under his pale skin and spoke, for the first time, something incomprehensible. Mother and father beamed benignly.

Gabor was a refugee from Budapest.

He was largely Father's doing. As I see it now, he was the sort of ideal foster-child he had always wanted; the answer to his forlorn, lugubrious, strangely martyrish prayers. Father had been an infantry officer during the war. He had been in North Africa and Normandy and at the liberation of concentration camps. He had seen almost all his friends killed around him. These experiences had given him the sense that suffering was the reality of life and that he had, in its presence, a peculiarly privileged understanding and power to reassure. Peace was for him a brittle veneer. He was not happy with his steady job in marine insurance, with the welfare state blandishments of those post-ration years. The contentments of fatherhood were equivocal. Now, as I look back, I see him waiting, watching over me, the corners of his stern mouth melancholically turned down, waiting for me to encounter pain, grief, to discover that the world was not the sunny playground I thought it to be; so that he could bestow on me at last—with love I am sure—the benefits of his own experience, of his sorrow and strength, the large, tobaccoey palms of his protection.

I must have hurt him. While he lived with his war-time ghosts, I was Richard Todd as Guy Gibson, with an RT mask made from my cupped hand, skimming ecstatically over our back lawn to bomb the Möhne Dam; or Kenneth More as Douglas Bader, cheerily cannonading the Luftwaffe.

Father scanned the newspapers. At headlines of trouble and

disaster he looked wise. When the news broke of the uprising in Hungary and its suppression, and later the stories of orphaned Hungarian children of my generation coming to our shores, who needed to be found homes, he acquired a new mission in life.

I did not take kindly to Gabor's arrival. Though he was not a proper adoption and was to be with us at first only on what the authorities called a 'trial basis', I was envious of him as a substitute child—a replacement of myself. A minor war, of a kind unenvisaged, between England and Hungary, might have ensued in our house. But I saw how—from the very start—I had a facility with Gabor which my parents did not, and the pride I derived from this checked my resentment. Besides, Gabor had the appeal of someone who—like my father—had lived through real bloodshed and conflict, though in this case the experience was of the present, not of the past, and belonged moreover to a boy my own age. Perhaps—unlike my father—he would share in, and enhance, the flavour of my war games.

This, should it be the case, would assuage another longstanding grievance against my father. I could not understand why, seasoned veteran as he was, he did no participate in, at least smile on my imaginary battles. I began to regard him as a bad sport and—more serious—to doubt his own quite authentic credentials. I tried to see in my father the features of my cinema heroes but failed to do so. He lacked their sunburned cragginess or devil-may-care nonchalance. His own face was pasty, almost clerical. Consequently I suspected that his real exploits in the war (which I had only heard about vaguely) were lies.

The first lesson in English manners I taught Gabor was how to shoot Germans.

When I reflect on this, it was remarkable that he grasped what was required of him. Not only did he scarcely know a word of English, but there was an historical difficulty. I had absolutely no knowledge of Hungary's role in the Second World War I)

was ignorant of its collaboration with the Nazis), which I took
to be a national duel between England and Germany. Nonetheless, when the smoke from our Bren guns or hand grenades had
cleared, and I informed Gabor, after bravely reconnoitering, of
another knocked-out Panzer, another slaughtered infantry patrol,
he would look up at me with implicit trust and grin, manically,
jubilantly.

'*Jo,*' he would say. 'Good, good.'

Father was horrified at the careless zeal with which Gabor took
part in my games. He could not understand how a boy who had
known real violence, whose own parents (for all we knew) had
been brutally killed, could take part so blithely in these fantasies.
Some impenetrable barrier—like a glass wall which gave to my
father the forlorn qualities of a goldfish—existed for him between
reality and illusion so that he could not cross from one to the other.
But it was not just this that distressed him. He saw how Gabor
looked to me and not to him, how when he returned from our
forays at the end of the garden Gabor would follow me like a
trusted commander; how, from the very beginning, that affinity
which he had hoped to have with this child of suffering had
eluded him. I often wondered how they managed together on the
first day, when father had gone up to 'collect' Gabor, like some
new purchase. I pictured them coming home, sitting mutely on
opposite seats in the train compartment as they bounced through
suburbia, like two lost souls.

'Gabor,' father would say as he lit his cigarette after dinner,
with the air of being about to make some vital announcement or
to ask some searching question.

'*Igen?*' Gabor would say, 'Yes?'

Father would open his lips and look into Gabor's face, but
something, some obstacle greater than that of language, would
leave his words trapped.

'Nothing.'

'Yes?'

Gabor would go pink; his eyes would swivel in my direction.

Later, when Gabor had acquired a little more English, I asked him whether he liked my father. He gave a rambling, inarticulate answer, but I understood it to mean from the manner in which it was spoken that he was afraid of him. 'Tell me about your own mother and father,' I asked. Gabor's chin trembled, his lips twisted, his eyes went oily. For two days not even the prospect of Messerschmitts to be shot down persuaded him to smile.

Gabor went to my primary school with me. Except when he had special language tuition he was scarcely ever out of my company. He was an intelligent boy and after eighteen months his English was remarkably fluent. He had a way of sitting in the class with a sad expression on his face which made all the teachers fall for him. I alone knew he was not really sad. My closeness to him gave me a superior standing among my English friends. Gabor would now and then mutter phrases in Hungarian because he knew this gave him a certain charisma; I would acquire even more charisma by casually translating them. In our newly-built brick school, with its grass verges and laburnums, its pictures of the Queen, maps of the Commonwealth and catkins in jam-jars, there was very little to disturb our lives. Only the eleven-plus hung, like a precipice, at the end of it all.

In the summer holidays Gabor and I would play till dark. At the end of our garden were the ramshackle plots of some old small holdings, and beyond them open fields and hedges sloping down to a road. These provided limitless scope for the waging of all types of warfare. We would scale the fence at the end of the garden, steal venturously past the tumbled sheds and smashed cucumber frames of the small holdings (still technically private property) and into the long grass beyond (later they built a housing estate over all this). At one point there was a sizeable crater in the ground, made by an actual flying-bomb in the war, filled with old paint cans and discarded prams. We could crouch in it and pretend we were being blown up; after each grisly death our bodies would be miraculously reconstituted. And everywhere, amongst the brambles and ground-ivy, there were little oddities and discoveries, holes, tree-stumps, rusted tools, shattered porcelain, debris of former existences (I believed it was this ground-eye view of things which adults lacked), which gave to our patch of territory infinite imaginary depths.

A few impressions are sufficient to recapture that time: my mother's thin wail, as if she herself were lost, coming to us from the garden fence as the dusk gathered: 'Roger! Gabor!'; Gabor's hoarse breath as we stalked, watching for enemy snipers, through the undergrowth, and the sporadic accompaniment, as if we shared a code, of his Hungarian: '*Menjünk! Megvárj!*'; Father, trying to restrain his anger, his disappointment, as we trailed in finally through our back door. He would scan disapprovingly our sweaty frames. He would furrow his brows at me as if I was Gabor's corruptor, and avoid Gabor's eyes. He would not dare raise his voice or lay a finger on me because of Gabor's presence. But even if Gabor had not been there he would have been afraid to use violence against me.

Father would not believe that Gabor was happy.

In the summer in which I waited with foreboding to hear the result of my eleven-plus, and Gabor also waited for his own fate to be sealed (he had not sat the exam, the education committee deciding he was a 'special case'), something happened to distract us from our usual bellicose games. We had taken to ranging far into the field and to the slopes leading down to the road, from which, camouflaged by bushes or tall grass, we would machine-gun passing cars. The July weather was fine. One day we saw the motor-bike—an old BSA model (its enemy insignia visible through imaginary field-glasses)—lying near the road by a clump of hawthorn. Then there was the man and the girl, coming up one of the chalk gulleys to where the slope flattened off— talking, disappearing and reappearing, as they drew level with us, behind the banks and troughs of grass, like swimmers behind waves. They dipped for some time behind one of the grass

billows, then appeared again, returning. The man held the girl's
hand so she would not slip down the gulley. The girl drew her
pleated skirt between her legs before mounting the pillion.

The motor-cycle appeared the next day at the same time, about
five in the hot afternoon. Without saying anything to each other,
we returned to the same vantage point the following day, and our
attention turned from bombarding cars to stalking the man and
the girl. On the fourth day we hid ourselves in a bed of ferns
along the way the couple usually took, from where we could just
see, through the fronds, a section of road, the top of the gulley
and, in the other direction, at eye level, the waving ears of grass.
Amongst the grass there were pink spears of willow herb. We
heard the motorbike, heard its engine cut, and saw the couple
appear at the top of the gulley. The girl had a cotton skirt and a
red blouse. The man wore a T-shirt with sweat at the armpits.
They passed within a few feet of our look-out then settled some
yards away in the grass. For a good while we saw just the tops of
their heads or were aware of their presence only by the signs of
movement in the taller stems of grass. Sounds of an indistinct
and sometimes hectic kind reached us through the buzzing bees
and flies, the flutter of the breeze.

'*Mi az?*' whispered Gabor. '*Mit csinálnak?*' Something had
made him forget his English.

After a silence we saw the girl sit up, her back towards us. Her
shoulders were bare. She said something and laughed. She tilted
her head back, shaking her dark hair, raising her face to the sun.
Then, abruptly turning round and quite unwittingly smiling
straight at us as if we had called her, she presented to us two white,
sunlit, pink-flowered globes.

On the way back I suddenly realised that Gabor was trying not
to cry. Bravely and wordlessly he was fighting back tears.

It so happened that that day was my parents' wedding anni-
versary. Every July this occasion was observed with punctilious
sentimentality. Father would buy, on his way home from work,
a bottle of my mother's favourite sweet white wine. My mother

would cook Steak au Poivre or Duck à l'Orange and put on her organdie summer frock with bits of tulle around the neckline. They would eat. After the meal my father would wash up, sportingly wearing my mother's frilled apron. If the evening was fine they would sit outside, as if on some colonial patio. My father would fetch the Martell. My mother would put on the gramophone so that its sound wafted through the open window, *Love is a Many Splendoured Thing* by Nat King Cole.

In previous years, given an early supper and packed off to bed, I had viewed this ritual from a distance, but now, perhaps for Gabor's sake, we were allowed to partake. Solemnly we sipped our half-glasses of sweet wine; solemnly we watched my parents. Inside, we still crouched, eyes wide, amongst the ferns.

'Fifteen years ago,' father explained to Gabor, 'Roger's Mother and I were married. Wed-ding ann-i-versary,' he articulated slowly so that Gabor might learn the expression.

I looked at Gabor. He kept his head lowered towards the table-cloth. His eyes were dry but I could see that at any moment they might start to gush.

Mother and Father ate their steaks. Their cutlery snipped and scraped meticulously. 'Gorgeous,' my father said after the second mouthful, 'beautiful.' My mother blinked and drew back her lips obligingly. I noticed that, despite her puffy dress, her chest was quite flat.

Gabor caught my eyes. Some sorrow, some memory of which none of us knew, could no longer be contained. Father intercepted the glance and turned with sudden heed towards Gabor. For the first time that evening something like animation awoke in his eyes. I could imagine him, in a moment or so, pushing aside the remainder of his steak, rejecting with a knitting of his brows the bottle of Barsac, the bowl of roses in the middle of the table, grasping Gabor's hand and saying: 'Yes, of course, this is all nonsense . . .'

But this was not to be. I was determined, if only to defy Father, that Gabor would not cry. There was something in our experience of that afternoon, I recognised, for which tears were only one response. Gabor relowered his head, but I pinned my gaze, like a mind-reader, on his black mop of hair, and now and then his eyes flashed up at me. A nervous, expectant silence hung over the dinner table, in which my parents resumed eating, their elbows and jaws moving as if on wires. I saw them suddenly as Gabor must have seen them—as though they were not my parents at all. Each time Gabor looked up I caught his eyes, willing them not to moisten, to read my thoughts, to follow my own glance as I looked, now at my father's slack jowl, now at Mother's thin throat.

Gabor sat in front of the window. With the evening light behind him and his head bent forward, his infant moustache showed distinctly.

Then suddenly, like boys in church who cannot restrain a joke, he and I began to laugh.

I learnt that I was to be accepted at a new grammar school. Gabor, by some inept piece of administration, was granted a place at a similar, but not the same institution, and arrangements were made for continuing his private tuition. The whole question of Gabor's future, whether or not he was to be formally adopted into our family, was at this stage 'under review'. We had till September to pretend we were free. We watched for the couple on their motor-bike; they did not reappear. Somehow the final defeat or destruction of the last remnants of the German army, accomplished that summer, did not compensate for this. But our future advance in status brought with it new liberties. Father, whose face had become more dour (I sometimes wondered if he would be glad or sorry if the authorities decided that he could legally be Gabor's 'father'), suggested that I might spend a day or two of our holiday showing Gabor round London. I knew this was a sacrifice. We had gone to London before, as a family, to show Gabor the sights. Gabor had trailed sheepishly after my parents,

showing a token, dutiful interest. I knew that Father had had a
dream once, which he had abandoned now, of taking Gabor by
himself up to London, of showing him buildings and monuments,
of extending to him his grown man's knowledge of the world,
his shrewdness in its ways, of seeing his eyes kindle and warm as
to a new-found father.

I took Gabor up on the train to London Bridge. I knew my way
about from the times Father had taken me, and was a confident
guide. We had fun. We rode on the Underground and on the top
decks of buses. In the City and around St Paul's there were bomb-
sites with willow-herb sprouting in the rubble. We bought ice-
creams at the Tower and took each other's photo in Trafalgar
Square. We watched Life Guards riding like toys down the Mall.

When we got home (not long before Father himself came in
from work) Father asked, seeing our contented faces: 'Well, and
how was the big city?' Gabor replied, with the grave, wise expression he always had when concentrating on his English: 'I
like London. Iss full history. Iss full history.'

DANNIE ABSE

Sorry, Miss Crouch

Whenever my father tucked the violin under his chin and dragged the wavering bow across the strings, his whole countenance would alter. Often with eyes half closed like a lover's, he would lean towards me and play Kreisler's *Humoresque* with incompetent daring. He was an untutored violinist who, losing patience with himself, would whistle the most difficult bits. I always liked to hear him play the wrong notes and whistle the right ones: and, best of all, I liked his response to my huge, small applause: he would solemnly and elaborately bow. After this surprising theatrical grace he would generally give me an encore.

That August evening he gave me several encores: *Men of Harlech*, *My Yiddisher Mama* and *Ash Grove*. Afterwards he said, 'You'll be ten next month—wouldn't you like music lessons?'

I was being offered a birthday present. Psss. I wanted a three-spring cricket bat, like the one M. J. Turnbull, the Captain of Glamorgan, used, not music lessons. I didn't want to play a violin.

'The piano,' my father said. 'We have a first class piano in the front room and nobody in the house uses it. Duw, it's like having a Rolls Royce without an engine. Useless. If your mother wants something for decoration she can have an aspidistra.' He replaced his violin in its case. 'Yes,' he continued. 'You can have lessons. You'd like that, wouldn't you, son?'

'No, don't want any,' I said firmly.

'All right,' he said, 'we'll arrange for Miss Crouch to come and give you piano lessons every Thursday.'

When my mother told me I could have a cricket bat as well, I was somewhat mollified. Besides, secretly, I was hoping Miss Crouch would look like a film star. Alas, several Thursdays later I discovered I disliked piano lessons intensely and mild, thin, tut-tutting Miss Crouch did not resemble Myrna Loy or Kay Francis. The summer was almost over and on those long Thursday evenings I wanted to be out and about playing cricket with my friends in the park. So, soon, when Miss Crouch was at the front door, her pianist's hand on the bell, I was doing a swift bunk at the back, my right, cunning cricket hand grasping the top of the wall that separated our garden from the back lane. My running footsteps followed me all the way to Waterloo Gardens with its minnow-smelly brook and the pointless shouts of other children in the cool suggestions of a September evening. In the summerhouse my penknife wrote my first poem—I expect it's still there—MISS CROUCH IS A SLOUCH.

My father was uncharacteristically stern about me ditching Miss Crouch. For days he grumbled about my lack of politeness, insensitivity and musical ignorance. 'He's only ten,' my mother defended me. On Sunday, he was so accusatory and touchy that when all the family decided to motor to the seaside I said cleverly, 'Can't come, I have to practise for Miss Crouch on the bloomin' piano.' They laughed, I didn't know why. And now even more annoyed I resolutely refused to go to Ogmore-by-Sea.

'We'll go to Penarth,' my father said, a little more conciliatory. 'I'll fish from the pier for a change.'

'Got to practise scales,' I said pushing my luck.

'Right,' my father suddenly snapped. 'The rest of you get ready, that boy's spoilt.'

My mother, of course, would not hear of them leaving me, the baby of the family at home on my own. However, I was stubborn and now my father adamant. Unwillingly, my mother, at last, planted a wet kiss on my sulky cheek and the front door banged

with 'goodbyes' and 'we won't be long'. Incredible—hard to
believe such malpractice—but they actually took me at my word,
left me there in the empty front room, sitting miserably on the
piano stool. 'What a rotten lot!' I said out loud and brought my
two clenched fists on to the piano keys to make the loudest
noise the piano, so far, had ever managed to emit. It seemed
minutes before the vibrations fell away, descended, crumbled,
into the silence that gathered around the tick of the front room
clock. Then, as I stood up from the piano stool, the front door
bell rang and cheerfully I thought, 'They've come back for me.
This time I'll let them persuade me to come to Penarth. I'd
settle for a special ice-cream, a banana split or a peach melba.
Maybe I'd go the whole hog and suggest a Knickerbocker
Glory. Why not? It hadn't been *my* idea to learn the piano as a
birthday present. Not only that, *they* had abandoned me, and in
their ten minutes of indecision I could have *died*. I could have
been *electrocuted* by a faulty plug. I could have fallen down the
stairs and broken *both my legs*. It would have served them right.'

I opened the front door to see my tall second cousin. Or was
Adam Shepherd my third cousin? Anyway, we were related
because he called my mother Auntie Katie and he, in turn, was
criticised with a gusto only reserved for relatives. Father had indicated he was the best-looking member of the Shepherd family
(excluding my mother of course), but he was girl mad. 'Girl
mad,' my mother would echo him, 'He needs bromides.'

Standing there, though, he looked pleasantly sane. And, suddenly, I needed to swallow. I would have cried except big boys
don't cry. 'What's the matter?' he asked, coming into the hall
breathing in its sweet biscuity smell. I told him about Miss
Crouch and my birthday, about piano scales and how I had
scaled over the wall, about them leaving me behind, the rotters.

'Get your swimming stuff,' Adam interrupted me. 'We'll go
for a swim in Cold Knap, it'll be my birthday present to you.'

'Can we go to Ogmore, Adam?' I asked.

Less than a half hour later in Adam Shepherd's second-hand

bull-nosed Morris we had chugged out of Ely and now were in
the open country. Adam was really nice for a grown-up. (He was
twenty-one.)

'Why do girls drive you crazy?' I asked him.

It was getting late but people were reluctant to leave the beach.
There was going to be one of those spectacular Ogmore sunsets.
Adam and I had dressed after our swim and we walked to the
edge of the sea. There must still have been a hundred people
behind us, spread out like a sparse carnival on the rocks and sand.
We were standing close to the small waves collapsing at our feet
when suddenly a man began singing a hymn in Welsh. Soon a
group around him joined in. Now those on the other side of the
beach also began to sing. Everybody on the beach, strangers to
each other, all sang *together*. When the man who had begun singing
sang on his own the hymn sounded sad. Not now. The music was
thrilling and I wished I could play the piano—if only one could
play without having to practise.

Adam kept telling me that those on the beach were behaving
uncharacteristically. 'Like stage Welshmen,' he said. 'This is like
a pathetic English B film. It's as if they've been rehearsed.' But
then Adam himself joined in the hymn. In no time at all, somehow, he was next to a pretty girl who was singing like billyo.
I had noticed how he'd been glancing at that particular girl even
before we went swimming.

'You look like a music teacher,' he said to the girl and he
winked at me. Consulting me, he continued, 'She doesn't look like
Miss Crouch, I bet?'

'Miss Crouch, who's she?' the girl asked.

Their conversation was daft. I gave up listening and threw
pebbles into the waves. I thought about what Adam said—about
the singing, like in a film. I had been to the cinema many times.
I'd seen Al Jolson. And between films, when the organ suddenly
rose triumphantly from the pit, it changed its colours just like the

sky was slowly doing now—the Odeon sky. Amber, pink, green, mauve. My mother had a yellow chiffon scarf, a very yellow scarf, and she sometimes wore with it an amber necklace from Poland. I don't know why I thought of that. I thought of them anyway, my parents, and soon they would be returning from Penarth. It was getting late. I went back to Adam and to the girl whom he now called Sheila. 'I'm hungry, Adam,' I said. 'We ought to go home.'

Adam gave me money to buy ice-cream and crisps so I left them on the beach and I climbed up on the worn turf between the ferns and an elephant-grey wall. At the top, on the other side of the road, all round Hardee's Café, sheep were pulling audibly at the turf. One lifted its head momentarily and stared at me. I stared it out.

I took the ice-cream and the crisps and sat on a green wooden bench conveniently placed outside the café. Down, far below, the sea was all dazzle, black and gold. Nearer, on the road, the cars, beginning to leave Ogmore now, had their side-lamps on. Fords, Austin 7s, Morris Cowleys, Wolseleys, Rovers, Alvises, Rileys, even a Fiat. I was very good at recognising cars. Then I remembered my parents and felt uneasy. If they returned from Penarth and found me missing, after a while they'd become cross. I'd make it up to them. I'd practise on the piano. I'd tell them about the singing at Ogmore. They'd be interested in that. 'Everybody sang like in a film, honest.'

When I returned to the beach the darkness was coming out of the sea. All the people had quit except Adam and Sheila. It seemed she had lost something because Adam was looking for it in her blouse. They did not seem pleased to see me. Unwillingly they stood up and for a moment, gazed towards the horizon. A lighthouse explosion became glitteringly visible before being swiftly deleted. It sent no long message to any ship, but another lighthouse, further out at sea, in the distance, nearer the Somerset coast, brightly and briefly replied.

'They'll be worried 'bout me,' I said to Adam.

'They'll be worried about him at home,' Adam told Sheila.

She nodded and took Adam's hand. Then my big cousin in a very odd, gentle voice. 'You go to the car. We'll follow you shortly.'

So I left them and when I looked back it was like the end of a film for they were kissing and any second now the words THE END would appear. I waited inside the car for *hours*. Adam was awful. Earlier he had been nice, driven me to Ogmore, swum with me, messed around, played word-games. Ice-cream. Crisps. It was the girl, I thought. Because of the girl he had gone mad again, temporarily. When he did eventually turn up at the car, on his own, pulling at his tie, he never even said 'Sorry!'

Returning to Cardiff from Ogmore usually was like being part of a convoy. There'd be so many cars going down the A48. And we'd sing in our car—*Stormy Weather* or *Mad About the Boy* or *Can't Give you Anything but Love, Baby*. But it was late and there were hardly any cars at all. Adam didn't even hum. He seemed anxious. 'Your father and mother will bawl me out for keeping you up so late,' he said.

Yes, it was *years* after my bed time. If I hadn't been such a big boy I would have had trouble keeping my eyes open.

'We'll have to tell them we've been to Ogmore,' said Adam gloomily, 'we'll have to say the car broke down, OK?'

Near Cowbridge, we overtook a car where someone with a hat pulled down to his ears was sitting in the dickey. We followed its red rear light for a mile or two before passing it. Then we followed our own headlights into the darkness. There was only the sound of the tyres and the insects clicking against the fast windscreen.

Adam wished we were on the phone. So did I. David Thomas, my friend, was on the phone. So were Uncle Max and Uncle Joe, but they were doctors. You needed a phone if you were a doctor. People had to ring up and say, 'I'm ill, doctor, I've got measles.' I wished we had a phone rather than a piano.

'Have you a good span?' I asked Adam.

'Mmm?'

'To play an octave?'

At last we arrived in Cardiff, into its mood of emptiness and

Sunday night. Shops dark, cinemas and pubs all closed. At Newport Road we caught up with a late tram, a No. 2A, which with its few passengers was bound for the terminus. Blue-white lights sparked from its pulley on the overhead wires. After overtaking it we turned left at the White Wall and passed St Margaret's Church and its graveyard where sometimes David Thomas and I would play hide-and-seek.

'Albany Road,' I said.

'Right,' said Adam. 'Don't worry. Don't say too much. I'll come in and explain about us having a puncture.'

'What puncture, Adam?' I asked.

He parked the car, peered at his wrist-watch under the poor lamplight. 'Christ, it's twenty to eleven,' he groaned. He needn't worry, I thought. When I told them that from now on I'd practise properly they would let us off with a warning.

When Adam rang the bell the electric quickly went on in the hall to make transparent the coloured glass of the leadlights in the front door. Then that door opened and I saw my mother's face . . . *drastic*. At once she grabbed me to her as if I were about to fall down. 'My poor boy,' she half sobbed.

In our living-room she explained how worried they had all been. They had made an especial point in returning early from Penarth and I had . . . 'Gone . . . *gone*,' said my mother melodramatically. Later it seemed they had all searched for me in the streets, the back lanes, the park, and she had even called at David Thomas's house to see if I was there.

'You didn't have to run off just because you don't like piano lessons,' my mother said scolding us.

'I don't like piano lessons,' I said, 'but—'

'He didn't run off,' Adam said, interrupting me. 'We had a puncture, Auntie.'

When my mother told Adam that, as a last resort, they had all gone to the police station, and that's where they were now, Adam became curiously emotional. He even made an exit from our living room backwards. 'Gotter get back,' he muttered, 'I'm sorry, Aunt Katie.' Poor Adam, girl-mad.

Before I went to bed my mother gave me bananas and cream and she mashed up the bananas for me like she used to—as if I were a kid again.

'I'll speak to your father about the piano when he comes in,' my mother said masterfully. 'Whatever he says, no more piano lessons for you. So don't fret. No need to run away again.'

I was in bed and asleep before the family returned from the police station. And over breakfast my father, at first, didn't say anything—not until he had drunk his second cup of tea. Then he declared authoritatively, 'I'm not wasting any more good money on any damn music lessons for you. As for the damn piano, it can be sold.' My father said this looking at my mother with rage as if she might contradict him. 'If this dunce, by 'ere,' he continued, 'can't learn the piano from a nice lady, a capable musician like Miss Crouch, well not even Solomon could teach him.'

My mother laughed mockingly, 'Ha ha ha, Solomon! Solomon was wise but he never played the piano. Ha ha ha, Solomon indeed, ha ha ha. Your father, I don't know.'

'Why are you closing your eyes?' I asked my father.

It was time to go to school. I had to kiss Dad on the cheek. As usual, he smelt of tobacco and his chin was sandpaper-rough. But he ruffled my hair, signifying that we were friends once more.

'I hate Mondays,' I said.

'Washing day. I loathe them too,' said my mother.

Miss Crouch never came to our house again. And it was almost a week before Dad took down his violin and played *Humoresque*. I didn't listen properly. I was waiting for him to finish so that I could ask him if, after we had sold the piano, we could have a telephone installed instead—like they had in David Thomas's house.

PATRICK SKENE CATLING

Beyond Blarney

Supine, then lowered vertiginously head downward, Ed Muskerry, late of *The Brooklyn Echo*, stared with bulging eyes at the grey sky of County Cork below him and the green trees and green meadow above. He had sworn that when he arrived in Ireland he would kiss the authentic, difficult Blarney Stone, the sill of one of the machicolations on the south side of the battlements of the keep of Blarney Castle, not the more easily accessible stone that the tourists usually kiss. After nearly forty years as a New York newspaperman, he felt that he needed all the help he could get to improve his prose style. If he had to risk his neck hanging upside down to kiss the Blarney Stone, so be it.

Ed Muskerry was a pilgrim come to his ancestral home and he was determined to do things right. He had already done—he had paid to have done —the research into his genealogy. Wasn't Cormac Laidhir MacCarthy, who built the original part of the Castle in the Fifteenth Century, a lord of Muskerry? Ed had his handsomely ornamented family tree at the pub, and wasn't that called the Muskerry Arms? There was even a Muskerry golf course—eighteen holes.

First he sought eloquence and fluency; then he would look for the perfect place for the composition of his family history and his memoirs. He fondly envisioned a thickish book, possibly bound in leather. He had looked forward to this undertaking throughout the last long years of reporting the often squalid and sometimes

horrendous police news of New York City. Now he aspired to
magic and poetry, and, if he ever regained an upright position,
to a pint of Guinness.

The top of the drink was like the full Moon. The rest of it
was as black and soft and mild as a West Cork night after the
Moon has set, early in the Springtime of the year.

'Fit for the mighty Cuchullain!' Ed jovially exclaimed, trying
out the blarney for the benefit of a tubby fellow with a red face
standing beside him in the bar. Ed lifted his glass mug as though
toasting the whole pantheon of the heroes of the Irish nation.
'Suitable for a celebration of the one hundred and first victory of
Conn of the Hundred Battles! Worthy of the wise Brian Boru of
the Tributes himself!'

'OK!' the other man said, raising his gin and tonic in courte-
ous response.

'The gentleman is Dutch,' the barman explained to Ed. 'He's
the one driving the white Mercedes. You probably noticed it as
you came in. A grand car.'

The Dutchman finished his drink with a gulp and indicated
with a quick forefinger that Ed and he would have more. Ed
smiled and raised his hand in friendly protest.

'No,' he said. 'Let me do this. Please. After all, this is my
country.'

'Oh, are you in property yourself?' the barman asked, as he
filled a fresh glass with ice-cubes. 'Herr Stuyvesant bought two
hundred acres this week. The other side of Kinsale. He showed
me a photograph of it—it's lovely. On the coast, of course. He
specialises in the coastal areas. That's funny really, isn't it? You'd
think with all their dykes they'd want to be inland for a change.'
The barman allowed himself a short laugh at his little joke and
then composed his face into an expression of serious respect for
money.

'But the coast is the thing to get hold of, isn't it? What do you
think Herr Stuyvesant paid for his latest bit? Six hundred and
forty thou. And he got a bargain, if you ask me. Next year it'll

be double, for sure, won't it? Our land has become much more valuable, thank God, since we got into the EEC. Do you remember before the vote, when many of the farmers were against joining?'

'No, I don't.'

'Sure, there were slogans painted on all the walls all over the countryside, and soon the farmers who did the painting will all be able to retire to luxury bungalows in Spain with fitted carpets and deep freezes full of steak.'

The barman slowly shook his head in awful admiration of the ways of the world and served the Dutchman his carefully prepared drink. He immediately began to drink it. The barman turned again to Ed. 'And for you it's another stout, is it?'

'Yes, please.'

'You're on holiday, are you?' the barman enquired.

'I have come to trace my ancestors,' Ed corrected him. 'I'm writing a book.'

'Oh. Writing a book. Well, there must be a lot of that going on, I suppose.'

'This *is* the land of Colum, Synge and Yeats,' Ed pointed out reproachfully. 'The land of the Gaelic revival. The land of the new Celtic cultural renaissance.'

The barman squirmed, as though his underwear had suddenly shrunk to an inadequate size.

'And the little people dancing in the fairy rings,' he added bitterly. 'But be fair. We're catching up fast. We have *Kojak* now, and Toyotas, and McDonald's, and *Star Wars*, and Mogadon, and—'

'I am looking for the Real Ireland,' Ed said with quiet dignity. He finished his Guinness. 'Thanks for the drink, Herr Stuyvesant. Take it easy, fellas. Goodbye now.'

Driving his Hertz Mustang back into the centre of Cork, Ed decided that he should take on local colouration that would enable him to blend with the surroundings and the inhabitants of the remote villages where he hoped to discover the Real Ireland. He

had seen groups of package holidaymakers emerging from the
big glassy sightseeing buses parked outside Jury's Hotel and he
was glad that he had eschewed that sort of companionship and
that mode of travel. What hope would he have had as an ordinary
tourist? He shuddered at the thought.

Over a mixed grill and a bottle of Beaujolais at the Oyster
Tavern, he decided that he must get some real Irish clothes as
soon as possible. As he sipped his second Irish coffee, he resolved
that he would do his best to set out on his journey of discovery
dressed like the late Barry Fitzgerald.

After lunch, Ed walked along Patrick Street, but found
nothing that seemed quite suitable in the windows of the unisex
boutiques. At last, however, in a narrow back street between
warehouses near the River Lee, he found a tailor's shop displaying
the right sort of tweed caps and dark brown shapeless suits. They
would have looked in place on market-day in a country town on
the far side of Finian's Rainbow in one of those antique Ealing
comedy love stories with folksy community sing-songs and jigs.

Dressed like a member of the cast of a road company doing
their best on a low budget to counterfeit *The Playboy of the Western
World*, Ed set forth in the general directions of Innishannon,
Timoleague, Glandore and a number of smaller and even more
sweetly beguiling villages, hamlets, crossroads and crooked turns
in unbeaten tracks that you can't miss if you get absolutely lost.

The Irish Tourist Board advertisements in *The New Yorker* and
other purveyors of superior fantasy had promised him that The
Emerald Isle had not been named unreasonably; but they had not
sufficiently prepared him for the degrees of greenness of its
greenery. Accustomed to the sparse, withered, ochreous-dun
patches of hibernating and not at all Hibernian grass in New York,
his eyes were amazed by the green greens of Ireland.

In the small fields and low hills and short stretches of strand
that rolled and twisted merrily past the windows of his car, in the
sunlight and shadows of that brisk, clear afternoon, these are a
few of the greens that he noticed: the greens of every class of

chlorophyllous vegetation (especially grass), moss green, olive green, jade green, lime green, peacock green, turtle green, finch green, gage green, bottle green, conifer green, pea green, pistachio green, Chartreuse green, *crème de menthe* green, Veronese green, Dufrenite green, the Brunswick green of oxychloride of copper, verdigris (the green of Greece), the greens of Malachite and Connemara marble, the green of thoughts in a green shade, the almost-black green of sea-wrack, the green of the pointed booteens of leprechauns, Kelly green, shamrock green and the green of the green flag of Eire.

The rural Irish greening of Edmond Muskerry made him feel more yearningly romantic than ever about the land of his fore-fathers. But where were his cousins? He longed to recognize personally the consanguinity that the professional genealogists' chart had seemed to guarantee. What is the romance of kinship if it is only a written testament, bloodless? Many of the more notorious literary romanticists of our era have demonstrated un-wittingly that it is nothing, less than nothing, a hole in time.

The sun was setting, casting almost horizontal amber beams, enriching still more the glorious greennesses of the landscape. Unfortunately, it appeared to be a landscape without figures. Furthermore, Ed had no more idea of his whereabouts than a *Chicago Tribune* war correspondent would have with Cubans in the African bush, though for utterly different reasons, of course. Ed had eaten only a Blarney ham sandwich for lunch, and his stomach was sending up spiral burblings of acid discontent.

Negotiating yet another abrupt corner, he came suddenly to the high, uneven, grey stone wall of what must have been an ancient demesne, a survivor of uncountable, half-forgotten skir-mishes, sieges, campaigns of attrition and social rearrangements. Surmounted by new barbed wire, the old wall ran on and on, above a deep ditch that looked like a moat, until, after half a mile or so, it came to a lodge and a pair of great black iron gates, flanked by massive stone pillars.

Ed stopped the car as close as possible to the side of the

narrow road and got out. On a large polished brass plaque on one pillar was inscribed the name, HINDSYTH HOUSE; on the other pillar, in meticulously painted red letters on white, a sign warned: 'Beware—Security System Fully Operational at All Times'. The estate of a hundred thousand welcomes! Ed thought sardonically. But his feelings of disorientation and hunger were stronger than his misgivings, so he rang the bell.

The response was immediate. Ed was startled by one of those loud, flat, mechanical voices that issue from intercom speakers in movies inspired by the works of Len Deighton, Richard Condon and so many others nowadays. The robot voice ordered Ed to state his business in English and to identify himself by displaying his credentials to an out-of-reach, downward-pointing small television camera, like the ones used to embarrass hold-up men in banks and to inhibit kleptomaniacal housewives in super-markets. In the Celtic lobe of his brain, Ed was slightly indignant, but, like most other people of our advanced culture, he never disobeyed machines. He took out his wallet and produced his old laminated *Echo* press card. The word PRESS was large and black enough to score many points with any robot properly pro-grammed to allow for the requirements of publicity. Within less than a minute a red Ferrari roared down the asphalt driveway and squealed to a halt just inside the gates.

The man who emerged from the shiny low car was a taller than average midget with lacquered, short, black hair, wearing beige vicuna and mohair plus-fours, a falconer's red leather gauntlet on his left hand, Gucci black loafers with silver-tipped tassels, and flashing cosmetic dentistry as white and even as a row of Chiclets.

The gates opened automatically, as they usually do in big-time novels about international dirty tricks.

'Hello, there, Ed!' the man exclaimed, shaking Ed by the hand. 'I'm Harry Hindsyth, accent on the second syllable. Call me Harry! How frightfully good of you to come by! I was just going to pop a bottle of bubbly. Come in, my dear chap, come in, do!'

In fact, that was who it actually was, none other than *the* Harry

Hindsyth, in the flesh, a creative artist within the meaning of the Act.

'I was wondering whether you could give me directions,' Ed began. 'My map-reading—'

'Of course, of course! No problem. All in the fullness of time. Jump in the old bus and we'll repair to the old manse and have a marvellous old gossip, eh? *The Brooklyn Echo*! My word! I'm tickled absolutely *pink*!'

Why not? Ed thought, for the name of the celebrated best-selling novelist had caused a light tremor, a *frisson*, of the journey-man journalist's excitement that somehow endures any number of years of drudgery, disappointment and disillusionment. Besides, there might be something to eat.

Soon they were seated in soft red leather armchairs in front of a realistic electric log fire in Harry's walnut-panelled study, with its stainless steel bar, its hi-fi entertainment centre and row upon row of all the editions of his exhaustively researched documentary fictional accounts of the political conspiracy, kidnapping, terrorism, blackmail, bribery, torture, assassination and trans-sexual incest and rape that make the world go round.

'Well, Ed, tell me now—what brings you to this neck of the woods?' Harry genially demanded when Ed was half-way through his first glass of champagne. 'Has one of my secretaries been talking? Perhaps I should make it quite clear that that report that I was training a chap in my rifle range to knock off the Prime Minister during question time to generate enthusiasm for my forthcoming opus was only a misinterpretation of a sort of feasibility study I was doing. I always insist that my yarns are a hundred per cent authentic. Anyway, nobody's proved anything, and I bet they never will. Is that what you came to see me about?'

Ed told of his self-assigned mission to search for the Real Ireland.

'All right, all right,' Harry interrupted with a knowing grin. 'I respect a man's right to secrecy. But really, as a matter of fact, if that's what you *are* looking for, the Real Ireland, I mean, you couldn't have come to a better place.'

'It's quite true. I really am.'

'Well, old boy, as you like. We'll play it your way. This is where it's happening. That Donleavy chap isn't the only creative artist concerned with his own immortality. I've already started building a mausoleum that's at least twice the size of his, and mine's bomb-proof. The literary centre has definitely shifted South-Westward since I moved here. Forget about Davie Byrnes's and Neary's and all that bogus palaver in Dublin. This is it. Go into Gerry Hegarty's place in Bantry and listen to the cultural chat. Go into Cronin's in Durrus—the gateway to the Sheep's Head Peninsula—any night of the week. Anna Cronin happens to be a very good friend of mine, if you'll forgive a bit of name-dropping. All the talk in her place these nights is about paperback rights, screen rights, foreign rights, the television series from the novelization of the film—you know, old boy, the nitty-gritty of the Irish literary life.

'Now that I'm here, everyone seems to have arrived. Len Deighton, Freddy Forsyth, everyone. There's Wolf Mankowitz in Ahakista—though, frankly, between you and me, his stuff's a bit esoteric for a plain chap like me. There's his neighbour What's-His-Name, who's just finished a novel set in Las Vegas. Young Nigel Slater has set up shop near Kilcrohane. I believe he's staked out part of the East African scene. Donald Grant is another star of the Kilcrohane galaxy. He specialises in arcane animal-husbandry tales and other autobiographical spin-offs. Marc Brandel's in Los Angeles at the moment, writing TV scripts, but of course he adores it here. Let's see, over in Ballydehob there's that Eric Somebody-or-Other—they say he's very sound on Danish fairy-tales. Sam Rathbone has taken up residence above Paddy Barry's bar in Durrus. Rathbone's writing-room is between the 'Ah, That's Bass!' sign and the sign for 'Hot Snacks'. We're expecting a lot from him. Do you see?

'And now, I'm afraid,' Hindsyth said, putting down his glass and getting to his tiny feet, 'you'll have to excuse me for an hour or so. The photographer's here. We're working on some rather marvellous electric hair-dryer commercials, even though my accountant hasn't as yet confirmed we're going to be able to get away with this project tax-wise. But modelling's an art as much as all the rest, don't you agree? Wait here. I'll be right back. I've got heaps more to tell you about my book.'

But Ed did not wait there.

A couple of days later he arrived back in New York. He was in time for St Patrick's Day. It was a great day for the Irish. He wore a small green cardboard bowler hat and a green carnation and drank green-dyed beer at P. J. Clarke's on Third Avenue, and then walked over to Fifth to watch the splendid parade. The bands played louder than ever. Never before had he seen such darling drum majorettes in such short green skirts. His eyes shone.

'At last!' he said.

ELIZABETH TROOP

Suicide at Malibu

Benito Pastmaster was going grey. His mistress, Esme Pastmaster, exclaimed about this frequently. They were very close.
It may be asked why Benito and mistress shared the same name—
Pastmaster. But only by those who do not know that in fact
Benito Pastmaster, in spite of the Italianate gigolo-sounding
name, was a large, ageing black poodle. They were a familiar
couple on the beach at Malibu, a stone's throw from Hollywood.
(Of course, how far a stone could be thrown was ceasing to have
any meaning for Benito, or indeed Esme. They were neither of
them as young as they had been.)

As they toddled along, they dreamed. Esme dreamed of the
days in Mittel-Europa and Shaftesbury Avenue, between the
Wars, when she had been a musical comedy star, all the rage.
Before Benito, before Malibu, she'd been, among other things, a
Princess. Polish, of course, but a Princess, no less. Her creamy
breasts and thighs had been lusted after by every eligible male in
his prime in those Lehar and Strauss years. Rich admirers offered
rubies and diamonds. They were accepted.

Benito's thought-processes were more olfactory. Smells in the
studios where he waited, when Esme had transferred her talents
(unsuccessfully) to the Silver Screen—the odd couplings with
other pampered pets around the azure swimming pools, when he
was a gay young dog.

Affectionate and tender, innocent *and* lucrative, thought Esme, looking back. All the blonde years, the milk and honey years.

It was hard even to lift one's leg at his age, thought Benito, who always seemed to have sand up his nose.

A blonde, but not always, not from the start. That first bottle of peroxide was bought daringly from the local chemist's shop when I was twelve, recalled Esme. In Burnley.

Burnley, hated Burnley, with its cobbled streets and clog-shod workers, clattering their early-morning way to the mills.

She would never be one of those, she swore. Was damned if she'd go into a mill with her voice.

That voice, which had been picked out in church choirs and infant classes and which pierced the neighbourhood as she practised, and drowned the wail of sirens calling the multitudes to work; that voice was going to pull her out of the mire, she was sure.

Her mother didn't go to the mill, preferring domestic service at the biggest house in the area. Oliver Clegg was the last in the line of a once powerful family; a bachelor of middle years. He was fond of young Esme. She found she could entice warm lozenges from his waistcoat pocket if she sat in his lap. (The family fortune had been founded on throat and chest lozenges, in this land of the bronchitic.)

Esme would sing with him, when he was in the mood to strike chords on the piano: 'Where e'er you walk, cool gales shall fan the gla-ade ... trees where you sit, shall crowd into a shade.' Esme's mother soon put a stop to that. When she said Mr Clegg had offered to pay for singing lessons she was forbidden to go there again.

'I'll never forget yon house,' she warned her ma. 'And I'll have one like it one day.'

Asked by a school chum how she would get one, she said men would give it to her. A man like Mr Clegg. Men paid ladies with beauty and talent. Like what? said her friend. Most people are afraid to know that, said Esme, but I'm not. Nutty as a fruit-cake, barmy, they called her, screwing their fingers into their temples and raising their eyes to heaven, to show how daft she was. It didn't do to get above yourself around there. The women had a quick flowering. Married young while the bloom was on them. However dank the houses each one emerged, virginally satin-sheathed, for her one bright day. Then came rounded bellies, soiled aprons and down-at-heel slippers. Part-time at the mill, kids running bare-bottomed in the alleys. Varicose veins and pulled-down mouths. 'But not for me,' sang Esme.

Esme bought sepia postcards of stage beauties, conned her mother into paying for elocution lessons, ninepence a week. She was no longer understood in the neighbourhood. Draped herself in the net curtains, crimped her hair, refused to eat chips and pease pudding and tried to enlarge her button breasts.

Esme, sixteen, ran off with a traveller in ladies' shoes. He was Manchester-based. Sampling one city, she desired another and took the train to London.

Her aunt, married to a baker in Kennington, put her up for a while, with the rest of her brood. Until she became the sequinned assistant of a magician at the local music hall—then she had to go. Her aunt washed her large, bony hands of her, saying she would come to no good.

Having had a long line of moral disapprovers already, Esme had only to think of them to return to the primrose path of non-virtue. She had never understood what was so bad about donating your body for pleasure, and so good about donating it for hard work. Crazy logic, she thought, shrugging her plump shoulders at her latest conquest. Women like her aunt, her mother—conformity took their youth and gave nothing back. Their men turned sour, beat or hated them—hers courted, cajoled and enjoyed her. So the sneerers acted like compost on Esme, activating her garden of delights. To Esme, joy was the only moral responsibility. Playing the dumb blonde was not so dumb. Making a virtue of necessity must be rewarded. Esme got hers.

During the Second World War Esme left for Hollywood with a small-part German actor with a toothbrush moustache. He had an uncanny resemblance to Hitler; without the latter's histrionic ability. In Hollywood he was restricted to valet parts, or third-rate gangsters. An expert in discomfiture (it was, in fact, real) he allowed, because of despair, any humiliation. As he cared little about class distinctions (being an aristocrat) he lost, for Esme, and for most people, any he might have had. She after all, only slept with gentlemen, not gentlemen's gentlemen. One of her principles.

With Jock she had to resign those principles. By this time, Benito, who at the time of her birth wasn't even a twinkle in his great great great grandfather's eye, was with her—had been with her, through all the green years and the lean years—her last male admirer.

Jock, she supposed, had saved her from despair. She could never really forgive him for that.

The studios had tried to make her over into various stars, a pseudo-Jeanette MacDonald—an ersatz Dietrich. They failed, reported cattily by the harridans of the gossip columns in *Movie Weekly* and *Star Secrets*. All she read, those days, having moved from her mock-Tudor Beverly Hills mansion to a shack on the beach at Malibu. She downed liquor, first from a glass, then from the bottle. Benito hated her to drink, hated following her zig-zag foot-steps along the deserted strand. Also he got glass in his paws from the broken bottles.

Jock met Esme after his abortive job with a hearty star who was not quite so virile as his parts suggested. Benito arranged this seemingly accidental event. He'd never seen himself as a canine cupid, but still, he told himself doggedly, something had to be done.

Jock McTavish had reached the Pacific coast after his disillusionment with his own depressed land. But the California Technicolor proved almost worse than the Scottish sepia. He had fled to the hearty star from the attentions of a voracious Hollywood hag-on-the-decline. Bed and board. Bed and bored. Bedded and boarded. He escaped, bumming his way around the

Los Angeles area: waiter, soda jerk, barman, bar-fly.

This was until the wiles of Benito Pastmaster, poodle extraordinary, changed his life.

Jock was washing dishes at a beachside hamburger joint used by the college surfing trade. Because Benito found food at the shack in short supply (Esme took liquid lunch, and dinner too) he frequented the back door of the joint, accepting scraps with a dignity suited to his advanced years. He was tolerated when the place was half-empty, when the evening disco crowds came he was ejected. He usually lurked in the environs of the garbage cans.

Jock, though disliking most animals, took to Benito because of his weary persistence. It reminded Jock of his own behaviour. Stubbornness was his major quality, too. Benito had by chance the one virtue that appealed to Jock.

Jock disliked the sycophantic attitude of most dogs, was delighted to find one who disproved the rule. They regarded each other with great respect. Benito didn't even give as much as a wag of the tail for scraps received. Neither did Jock.

Fellow survivors in the game of chance. We're still in there— Jock said to the mutt as he handed him hamburgers that had been toyed with and left by the over-fed youngsters.

Then came the time when Jock had to put his loyalty where his mouth was, so to speak. Benito was banned on grounds of hygiene. Jock suggested that with kitchens like theirs, they must be jesting. They fired him on the spot.

The end is unimportant, he said to Benito, as they huddled in a doorway in the unaccustomed rain. Persistence is all, friendship is all. He patted Benito's old head, which smelled of wet wool. Whereupon Benito led him home.

It was as if the dog had been working towards this all summer. He pushed open the door of the shack with his nose. After noting that Jock had followed him in, he curled up on a threadbare rug, turning three times in a sort of superstitious way. He seemed to expect no welcome.

Esme was sprawled on a day bed, covered in movie magazines

and astrological charts. Jock, leaning over for a better view, heard Benito growl. He recognised her; had seen her at the beach café sometimes, a blowsy blonde, usually the worse for wear. He had never connected her with Benito.

So Jock discovered his mission in life. Without suspecting it, he had swallowed Benito's bait.

Esme stirred, smiled and went back into her stupor again. Jock picked up a Mexican poncho from the floor, wrapped it around himself and did likewise. Whenever the cold dampness and the sea noises woke him he saw Benito's eyes on him, like two red coals in the dark.

Jock and Benito went to the restaurant at dawn next day and stole a French loaf from the doorstep and some oranges from the store room at the back. Jock had a key and he took what he regarded as his severance pay from the petty cash. They bought coffee and dog biscuits from Pepe's Cut-Rate Super Store on the way back. Benito, who hadn't seen a dog biscuit in years, was ecstatic. So this was the way it was going to be . . .

Back at the hut Jock scoured out a rusty kettle and put on water for coffee. Esme opened one eye to tell him the water was usable, in spite of what the notice above the faucet said. Then she slept again. By the time he had created a life-giving resurrection breakfast of orange juice, coffee and bread she was wide awake, showing few of the ravages of what must have been a heavy evening's drinking. He had stumbled on endless bottles under the sink as he searched for the kettle.

She rose. Fifty, sixty? He couldn't tell. Battered, but salvageable. He asked if he could move in with such quiet authority that, mollified by the breakfast, she agreed. First she asked Benito, who thumped his flea-infested tail on the floor.

They talked for hours, decided that what each of them wanted was to return to the Old Country. Benito pricked up his ears at that. They drank a toast to that.

Jock suggested carefully that sex should not have a major part in their relationship. Benito saw that although he had been quite careful in the way he phrased this, Esme's child-like face trembled as Jock skated over the thin ice of her vulnerability.

They had a good fall that year. Jock dried her out, he had made her admit it wasn't spirits but spirit she needed. He had to admit, Great Romantic though he was not, that she had lived a Life. In spite of himself he was thrilled that she had known Ivor and Noel, Counts and Princes, Ziegfeld and Billy Rose. Finally—the Hollywood saga. Then she sobbed. She had flopped—hitting it as she did at the coke-vitality, Grable and Faye time.

Off the bottle, slimmed-down, a new agent later, she took on bit parts. She got Jock a job in her old studio, Wardrobe Department. Nightly he brought home clothes for their new life. For himself two chauffeur's uniforms and a dress suit. For her, Ingrid Bergman-type gear, sporty but elegant, and a couple of evening dresses that had graced Grace Moore.

In this way, eating at the studio commissary, clothing themselves from Wardrobe, they stacked up dollars for the return home. Benito guarded the hat-box where the dollar bills nestled under ostrich feather-trimmed picture hats. A silver grey Rolls to match the chauffeur's uniforms was dreamed of, evenings, sitting on the beach, watching the tangerine sun go down.

Esme blossomed. Sought out old admirers who could be touched for a small role. She got quite a reputation as a character actress; soon Jock was wearing the chauffeur's gear for real, driving her to the studio in a second-hand Ford.

They never forgot their aim: London. It was something they both rather dreaded, having, it seemed, hit a winning streak at last. But they had an ideal: old age pensions, crumpets by the fire on blustery evenings. Nostalgia spurred them on.

Benito had been left to his own devices since they had been working so hard. Now, suffering from depression, it was suggested (in whispers) that he might visit one of the many dog-psychiatrists abounding in the area. Jock finally said no to this, it would cut into their savings too much. Benito punished them by failing to greet them when he heard the car draw up. After all, he had brought them together. He could only assume they would stick by him. They did seem touchingly concerned. His hearing was bad, but he thought he heard them discussing his adoption by someone kind—apparently he was too old to go into quarantine in the Old Country. Then he heard Esme say who in his right mind would want a fourteen-year-old poodle with chronic fleas, almost blind in one eye, with the disposition of a crotchety old man? It would be difficult, agreed Jock. Benito was mad at that, and pissed on their new rug.

One evening, they fed him royally, on steak, cut up into chewable pieces by Esme's red-tipped loving hands. Jock then measured him, saying it was for a new coat. But Benito had seen the baroque von Stroheim-type coffin they had smuggled in from the studio. It had been used for a pet chimp's funeral.

Benito gave Esme's pearly toenail a farewell lick, for old time's sake.

While they were dining *à deux*, dressed in their costumes, Benito toddled off to the ocean, the blue Pacific.

He was written up as the only known dog suicide in Malibu. Or indeed, anywhere else.

Having nothing to detain them, they now set sail from New York.

ROBERT NYE

The Facts of Life

'It is time,' said my grandmother, 'that the boy knew'.

I looked up from my jigsaw. I was ready for distractions. *The Boyhood of Raleigh* in one thousand two hundred and fifty pieces, and after three afternoons I had just this minute discovered that the sailor's finger had been missing from the start.

My grandmother was sitting rocking in the rocking chair with her back to us. It was an hour this side of Horlicks, and September, and outside the French window the sun was shining on the begonias. My grandmother should have been reading aloud the births and deaths and marriages and for sale. She liked to sit with the newspaper smooth across her lap, an apron of gossip, feeding us with titbits. Occasionally my mother would cluck her tongue when my grandmother's tone changed for a name or a price, but I don't think she was ever really listening.

'Ten,' said my grandmother. 'It is old enough.'

Perhaps they were not begonias, those flowers. I liked the word, though, and still do, though now I think it is a funny word, and then I didn't. To my young ear, it sounded like a beginning, or something a pale but animated girl might play upon the piano, having to cross her hands for the difficult bits. My grandmother had strict opinions about flowers. When, a little later, I wrote a sonnet about the Greek boy who fell in love with his own reflection, she insisted upon referring to it as my poem about the narcissi. She called the flowers begonias that grew outside the window, and so begonias they were. My grandmother, a widow, was a woman of character.

'When *my* Robert was ten he had sailed to Valparaiso.'

And had been up the topmast three times, I thought.

'And been up the topmast three times,' said my grandmother, rocking. 'In a storm,' she added, and I had not thought of that.

My mother knitted and said nothing. Her eyes were fixed upon the open-heart operation on the television. The Woodbine trembled on her lower lip. No doubt she thought that my grandmother was still reading aloud from the *Southend Standard*. I felt down the back of the sofa for the missing finger. The rocking chair stopped rocking.

'So tell me,' said my grandmother, 'what steps you intend to take'.

Interference zigzagged across our TV screen, spoiling my mother's pleasure in the first incision, making her drop a stitch. 'That Freeman's got his Black and Decker out again,' she said. 'It ought to be suppressed.' She was a quiet woman, my mother, but she took a close interest in televised surgery. She retrieved her stitch. 'Steps?' she said.

'His father,' said my grandmother. 'It would come better from him, wouldn't it? A thing like that.'

My mother averted her gaze from what Mr Freeman's Black and Decker drill was doing to the flesh upon the operating table. She looked at my grandmother. I had seen these looks before. 'Daddy', she said, nodding so that the cigarette snowed ash down upon her knitting. 'The best course by far.'

And so it was that the following Friday, after supper, my father put on his hat and took me out for a walk. This, I may say, struck me as unusual even at that time. In the first place, my father was not often to be seen with a hat on his head, on account of his dandruff treatment. In the second place, I could not recall that he had ever taken me for a walk before, not even when he came home from the war and my grandmother told me that we had won. I remember, to be fair, that he did give me a whole bar of milk chocolate, but he did not take me for a walk on that occasion.

It was a very long walk indeed. We went down Valkyrie Drive and along Westcliff Avenue and Prittlewell Avenue and Thorpe Bay Avenue and then up Chalkwell Park Road and right round the park including the cricket pitch and the putting green and the Garden of Remembrance. I cannot remember thinking anything in particular, except how proud I ought to be to be out walking with my father, and how glad I was that it was not raining and that none of my friends had seen us. Here we are, I thought to myself, a son and his father out walking on a fine Friday evening in September, man to man, stride for stride, just like *Life with the Lyons* or Abraham and Isaac or any normal family. When we had circumvented the cricket pitch and came to the Garden of Remembrance I added to this thought the observation that the sun was shining on the begonias. They were probably real begonias in the Garden of Remembrance, because I had heard my grandmother complimenting Old Smiley the park-keeper on the display and he had not denied it.

My father said nothing at all on the outward journey, but on the way back he took a deep breath in Chalkwell Park Road and cleared his throat in Thorpe Bay Avenue and Prittlewell Avenue and then again in Westcliff Avenue. All up Valkyrie Drive he was clearing his throat and taking deep breaths as if for a conversation, but it was not for a conversation, it was for athletics because abruptly as we drew level with the monkey puzzle tree in the garden of 46 he quickened his stride. I quickened my stride too. My father looked at me balefully out of the corner of his eye. He managed to add another inch to his stride as we got to the garages. He goose-stepped, in fact, all fleeing and flinging arms and legs, down Cranleigh Road, in the direction of our house. I broke into a trot, then sprinted, trying to keep up with him. It was no use. He burst away from me. His hat fell off and rolled in the gutter but he did not stop. He was a lamppost ahead when he reached our garden gate and headed up the path for the pink front door.

Before my father could get the key from his trouser pocket, the door opened. It was my grandmother. She had a carpet beater in her hand. She took one look at the two of us. We stopped in our tracks—or, to be precise, I stopped in my father's tracks, holding out his hat as though that would explain everything, while he stood gangling, shifting from foot to foot, gazing up critically at the roof as though he expected a tile to fall.

My grandmother called softly to my mother over her shoulder: 'He hasn't told him.'

'Listen,' said my father. 'Wait.'

My grandmother took one step forward and my father took two steps back.

'You tell him,' she said. 'Don't you dare bring that boy back till you've told him.' She slapped her side with the carpet beater. 'It's time he knew,' she said. 'When your father was his age he'd been round Cape Horn.' She turned and went into the house and slammed the door shut. Three times, I thought. 'Twice,' she screeched through the letterbox.

With a weary but manful sigh, my father turned and took his hat from my hand. He dusted it and put it on his head. Then he went to look at his reflection in the front room window to make sure that the hat was on straight. But my mother and grandmother were standing there behind the lace curtains waiting and watching, so my father spun round and grabbed me by the ear and then off we went away down Valkyrie Drive again.

I had less pleasure in the walking now. The sun had gone behind a cloud. In Prittlewell Avenue a fat man with no shirt on was snipping at his hedge with a pair of shears and the smell of the privet got up my nose and made me sneeze on and off all the way to the park. My father grunted and walked daintily. I think he was pretending that this sniffing, sneezing, long-legged brat in wide white shorts had nothing to do with him. For my part, I felt guilty. Whatever it was that my father was supposed to tell me no longer seemed important. What was important was that it was now getting too late for his game of brag at my uncle Oswald's. My father had not missed his Friday brag at uncle

Oswald's since the night when the chimney caught fire, and here
he was having to miss it because he was out walking me round
the streets of Southend-on-Sea because my grandmother would
not let us in until he had told me.

If I had been a cleverer boy I would have suggested that we
called it a day, and that we both retired to uncle Oswald's for a
game of brag. As it was, I shuffled and snuffled unhappily around
the putting green in my father's wake, wishing that I had a
handkerchief.

'Blow your nose,' he said, and then he started mumbling.

'Beg pardon?' I said.

'Blow your nose,' he said.

'No, not that,' I said, 'the other.'

We had reached the Garden of Remembrance, with its stone
that said that They would not grow old as we that were left grew
old, and that at the going down of the sun and in the morning we
would remember Them. I knew who They were. My grandfather
who had maybe been to Valparaiso and Cape Horn, before he
was my age, had without doubt been to Ypres and not come back,
before my father was born. He was gassed and he was dead in
No Man's Land, my grandfather, before he even knew that his
wife was going to have a baby.

I wiped my nose on the back of my hand. 'I haven't got a
hankie,' I explained.

My father looked at me. Then he fumbled in his pocket and
produced his own handkerchief. He unfolded it with care. Tears
started to my eyes. My father blew his nose and stuffed the handkerchief back where it had come from.

'You'll go mad,' he said. 'You'll go mad and all your teeth will
rot and your hair will fall out so that everyone will *know* and
you'll end up dribbling in a wheel chair.'

'Beg pardon?' I said.

My father fixed his gaze on the going down of the sun. 'I
speak of excess,' he said. '*Excess.*' He paused. His face shone.
Under the brim of the squashed hat his eyes were blazing hot. A

butterfly settled on his lapel. 'The damned thing,' he said, 'is unavoidable'. The butterfly warmed its wings on his brown serge. My father's hand came up trembling as if to touch it. I held my breath. I had never seen anyone stroke a butterfly, and my father was not a great stroker of any kind. If he strokes this creature, I thought to myself, I will *really* believe about God and the Virgin Mary, and Spike Langdon's dad and the au pair girl.

My father flexed his right forefinger against his thumb and flicked the butterfly into the begonias. '*Don't touch it*!' he hissed. 'That's all I have to say after a lifetime of experience.' He shut his burning eyes, and swayed on the balls of his feet. 'I found tennis some help,' he confided, 'when I was your age.' He opened one eye. 'Always remember', he said, 'it takes as much out of a man as three hard sets played in the mid-day sun.'

I was impressed. All the way back along Westcliff Avenue and Valkyrie Drive I thought about what my father had said. When we passed the monkey puzzle tree, I said, 'Dad.'

'Enough,' said my father.

'Yes,' I said. 'But——'

My father jammed his hat down over his ears and fell upon the garden gate like a Roman soldier falling upon his sword.

'But no buts,' he cried.

He swept past my mother and my grandmother in the hallway. 'Now he knows,' he said.

My grandmother looked at me. My mother looked at my grandmother. My grandmother looked away. 'No, he doesn't,' she said.

'Look, he wouldn't listen,' said my father, leaning on the banisters. 'I tried to tell him, but he wouldn't listen.'

My shoe lace was undone. I wanted to say that I was sorry, but the word wouldn't come out, so I did up my shoe lace instead.

'He just kept sniffing,' explained my father.

My grandmother shook her head. She looked at my mother. My mother looked at me.

'We know you don't know,' my mother said grandly, taking

the Woodbine from her mouth. 'You don't know and you don't
want to know. Well, now you'll never know. You'll go through
life and you'll never know. And that's an end of it.'

It wasn't.

J. E. HINDER

Just the Two of Us

Rupert had always indulged in at least three Night School classes every week, right back to the period after our discharge from the Balloons towards the end of the War—or the 'late hostilities' as he used to say during bouts of uncharacteristic jocularity. To tell the truth, there was little enough to occupy the evenings. Mother never let the cathode-tube past the front door of 'Cathchas', the Beau Brummell Picture Theatre was a hotbed of hooliganism and he never partook of the 'poisoned chalice'—another serio-comic description he was wont to employ. Yes, the pseudo-camaraderie of the saloon bar had little significant appeal to our Rupe, and, besides, he felt it his bounden, not to say moral, duty to avoid such places because of what Mother had suffered through Father's frailty, he having fallen away into an inebriate's grave when Rupert was six.

Dad left behind him the stone-built semi-detached residence known as Cathchas, Number 18, Mordred Road, the furniture therein, the works of the Swan of Avon and two widows, the second of whom was never mentioned within the walls of Cathchas, and whose name filial loyalty still forbids me to expose in print for the salacious delectation of what I must assume to be a mixed readership.

In earlier years Mother always frankly avowed she had never known a lad less avid of companionship than her Rupe. 'All company is bad company,' she was wont to aver, although in her

settled days she revealed no great antagonism towards a smatter-
ing of Night School. She often opined that when one or two
were gathered together for the purpose of education there was
small danger of 'unpleasantness', her sober synonym for sexual
pleasure. In fact, she likened it to chapel-going, although she
never exposed herself to outward religious observance after the
scandal of Dad's demise and, indeed, after that calamity, she
never set foot outside the familial dwelling. 'I put my trust in our
four-footed pals now,' she often declared. There were three cats
at first: Helen, Mary and Snuffly and after they were translated
to Higher Spheres there were three more: Porker, Baby Charlie
and Tinkerbell. Canine friends she eschewed, not because of any
antagonism but because of the difficulty of walking them through
streets frequented by human beings.

In her later years, after her health began to deteriorate, Mother
became unnaturally suspicious, poor old girl, especially, strange
to say, of that former apple of her eye, Rupe. By that time he had
risen to the lofty position of Assistant Accountant at Windgell
and Fern's, Corn Brokers, where bitter constraint and sad
occasion dear had long nudged him to earn his daily crust and
where he was, in fact, unanimously categorised as the dryest of
dry sticks. But Mother, in those later days, now less salad than
vegetable, cast continual aspersions concerning his hypothetical
conduct without the sheltering walls of Cathchas, aspersions
about which you may well, reader, wish to turn the business of
your souls to such exsufflicate and blown surmises, matching my
inference.

Mother's accusations at this sad period of her voyage, in
respect of our Rupe's association with this secretary, Miss Bailey
(a lady of fifty inclement summers and the sole support of a
demented cousin) made very forges of his cheeks, he admitted,
that did to cinders burn up modesty. Mother chose to regard the
sombre premises of Windgell and Fern as a modern Babylon,
populated by a plethora of Scarlet Women. At this time she had
become addicted to a low-class weekly mag. that delighted to re-

veal to its finger-reading subscribers the more sordid aspects of our society. To this journal she frequently drew his embarrassed attention late in the evening when he brought to her solitary cot the invariable cup of cocoa. 'With how many Jezebels like this do you toy during office-hours?' she would demand, indicating snaps of salaciously-stimulated females, many in a state of Nature.

It became the same with Night School. In these, her declining years, she became oppressed by visions of non-Caucasian males, declaring continually that she described ebon faces, peering at her sensually through the casements. 'How many Ethiops have you in your class?' she would cry and when, once, he weakly confessed that there were three highly-respectable black students attending First Year Italian, she accused him of inaugurating a perverse quadrilateral relationship, making use of language unprintable in any tongue other than Danish. Rupe was utterly nonplussed by her behaviour but, despite the cogent advice of sage Dr Pheasant, the family Medical Adviser, we resisted all efforts to have her confined within the walls of the under-staffed local Bedlam.

Two years ago, Mother passed away. Rupert was forty-six and his particular grief was of so flood-gate and o'er bearing nature that it was a full two months before he brought himself to return again to his evening studies and enrol in the Art of the Italian Renaissance, Leatherwork, Motor Maintenance and 1st Year German. It was at the latter class, shortly after his return to the World of Light, that he first encountered the woman Sylvie.

He had undergone a very trying week, what with the auditors being in and the last Quarter of the Moon and the onset of a heavy head cold of the type to which he had been a martyr since puberty. He had always been preternaturally coy when called upon to read aloud in class, so, no sooner had he ejaculated (by order of his instructress Fraulein Smirthwaite) 'Ich habe, du hast, er hat,' than he was taken queer and briefly lost consciousness. When he came to, he was immediately aware of an overpowering female fragrance and, looking up, saw to his horror, the upper section of a well-built woman hanging precariously above him. 'Speaking as a former SRN,' remarked Sylvie (for it was she!), 'I'd say you should push off home quicksticks! Your pulse is highly erratic.'

The upshot was (to miniaturise an over-sized narration) that this blonde person (35) elected against his feebly-expressed protests to drive him in his own Morris Minor to the homely shelter of Cathchas, where, upon arrival, after learning of his totally unmarried status, she entered the premises and demanded that he retire to his bachelor bed. Harried thus unwontedly by a person of opposing gender, he weakly acceded, only to collapse in a swoon on reaching the actual cot.

He awoke to find himself comfily tucked in between the sheets, clad in his best maroon pyjamas, while, sitting at the foot of the bed reading *Random Harvest* was his blonde benefactress. She demanded the name of his Club Quack and, after stating that she would summon Dr Pheasant to his bed of pain the next day, left the house. It was only then that our Rupe, an icy shiver running down his spine, realised the significance of his pyjama-clad state.

At the next meeting of 1st Year German, Sylvie boldly occupied the adjoining pew. After the lesson she openly asked him to take her out for nocturnal repast, adding that though conjugally united to a male person, she was, nevertheless, extremely unhappy in that state. All the way to the Golden Partridge, an eating-house confidently selected by his companion, Rupert was all of a sweat. In his mind's eye he saw his over-bold conduct proclaimed in letters of fire on the office walls at Windgell and Fern's. He heard the whining voice of the unfortunate Miss Bailey retailing his daring escapade to drooling Cousin Phoebe. Disgrace beckoned and he trembled like an aspen-leaf throughout the meal, while Sylvie, unperturbed, enumerated between minestrone and apple-tart with Ideal milk, the brutalities and sensualities of her marriage-partner, George.

The next week she turned up at class with a bruised eye and other contusions, invisible, she coyly hinted, in normally-permitted street-attire. She openly informed Rupe that her husband had returned home the previous night, fresh from the embraces of some unlettered wanton and had assaulted her, committing afterwards a certain action. On the way to the car-park after class she surprised Rupe by bestowing upon him an enveloping kiss, after which brazen attack he was flabbergasted to hear her suggest that she visit Cathchas itself the following evening. To his request the trembling Rupe (47) muttered a thoughtless affirmative. When he finally arrived home, faint and weary, he took a Disprin, some hot milk, let the cats in and had an early but sleepless night.

All next day, dire premonitions afflicted him, so that he actually made a mistake at the office and was roundly reprimanded by Mr Hockle, the Chief Accountant and by the newly-installed computer, Vardoc. His feelings were indescribable, and it must have been apparent to all that he was not up to scratch, for many of the younger members of the staff, surmising that Nature would not invest herself in such shadowing passion without instruction, declared that he had finally gone round the twist.

At this juncture, deeming that I had been silent too long, I realised I must take a hand. I knew the whole terrible story, of course, close to him as I was, so close. Yes, I had heard that Christian name oft muttered nocturnally into a moist pillow, I had watched the feet falter along the primrose path. It was time! I fought for his salvation until the hour of seven at which time my chaste injunctions finally bore fruit. It was the mention of Mother that did it. 'What of she,' I cried, 'who has now mercifully disentangled herself from this mortal coil?' and pointed to the tinted enlargement of a snap taken of the family near the Old Pier at Weston-super-Mare. 'See!' I shouted, 'see, how amazement on thy Mother sits!' Yes, at the mention of she who bore us (albeit reluctantly, considering the method of insemination human frailty ordains for us here below), our Rupe rained down salt tears upon the Axminster. 'Mother!' he sobbed. After two verses of *All things bright and beautiful* (her favourite hymn), it was decided.

I was to be the one to welcome her to her hoped-for bower of balmy bliss. I took over completely. False as Hell was the smile with which I greeted her at the door. False as Hell was my embrace. 'Darling!' she whispered, her snake-like arms round my neck. 'Darling!' I replied with indefatigable conviction as I took her rather thick neck between my hands and squeezed, gently at first, then very much harder . . .

. . . And so you lie there, Sylvie, pale as your smock, as the saying goes, looking as if you were alive, I swear, one shoe fallen from your foot, one special offer size seven in which you shall no more saunter through the sordid streets and subways or wander through the wilderness of this world. I had to take command, Sylvie, because he was weak. From poor Rupe, no deeds to make Heaven weep, all earth amazed. Surely you did not think that I, a true son of my Mother, would permit you to tempt Rupe into the Garden of the Hesperides in the holy dusk of her own Cathchas, to have it off within spitting distance of that bedroom where even the china wash-basin had been dedicated to purity? Never, Sylvie!

Of course, in life you never knew Mother, you were never vouchsafed that inestimable boon, indubitably cracked though she was in latter years, and I doubt if you twain will meet in that hollow vale because Mother never was much of a mixer and she won't have changed, she'll be keeping herself to herself still. I shan't say any more at the moment but perhaps I might get the opportunity for a chat later on—I'm just going to stop up the crack under the door, make sure the windows are air-tight and then turn on the gas-fire. Mother will be pleased to see us, Rupe and me. Oh, yes, Rupe's coming too. I mean, it's difficult to explain to an outsider, but . . . well, he's always accompanied me everywhere. Inseparable we've been, inseparable. So he's coming too. How can he help himself, Sylvie, how can he possibly help himself?

EDNA O'BRIEN

Mary

Dear Sadie,

I am on the toilet as it's the only place I get a bit of peace. She is calling me down to do the dinner as I am a good cook and she is not. He raised ructions yesterday about cabbage water and I got red and you won't believe it but he smiled straight into my face. He never smiles at her. If I tell you a secret don't tell anyone. She sees another man. Didn't I walk straight into them the night I was to meet Tom Dooley and he never came. Next day she gave me a frock of hers, I suppose so's I'd keep my mouth shut. And now I am in a fix because she expects me to wear it when I go dancing and I want to wear a frock of my own. It is brushed wool, mine is, and I know it is brushed wool, but I am not telling her.

Tom Dooley came the next night. He got the nights mixed up, a good job I was there. We went for a walk in the park opposite this house—there's a park, I told you that, didn't I? It's nice in the summer because there's a pavilion where they sell ice cream and stuff but dead boring in the winter. Anyhow we had a walking race through the woods and he beat me blind and I got so winded I had to sit down and he sat next to me and put his arm around me. Then he kissed me and all of a sudden he raised the subject of SEX and I nearly died. I got such a fright that I took one leap off the seat and tore across the field and he tore after me and put his arms around me and then I burst out crying, I don't know why. And I had to come in home and when I did he was here by himself. She's always out. Goes to pubs on her own or wandering around the road gathering bits of branches saying how sad and how beautiful they are. Did you ever hear such nonsense in all your life. She wouldn't darn a sock. Anyhow he was here listening to music. He always is. And he called me in to warm my feet and sat me down and we hardly said one word except that he asked me was I all right and I had to say something, so I said I got a smut in my eye. Didn't he get an eye-glass and was poking away at it with a little paint brush and didn't she come in real quiet in her crepe-soled shoes.

'Oh, togetherness,' she said in her waspy voice and you wouldn't see me flying up the stairs to bed. Next morning—and you mustn't breathe this to a soul—she was up at cock-crow. Said she had heartburn and went out to do some weeding. It's winter and there's nothing in those flower beds only clay. Guess what, wasn't she waiting for the postman and no sooner had he come than she was all smiles and making coffee and asking me what kind of dancing I like, and didn't the phone ring and when she tripped off to answer it I had a gawk at the letter she got. I could only scan it. Real slop. It was from a man. It said darling be brave. See you a.m. Now I haven't told you this but I love their child. He has eyelashes as long as daisies and lovely and black. Like thread. I admired them one day and he wanted to pull one out for me. I'd do anything for that kid.

Anyhow I discovered where she keeps the letters—under the hall carpet. She presses flowers there too. Of course if I wanted to, I could show them to hubby, find them, pretend I didn't know what they were. I'm not sure whether I will or not. I heard him telling her once that he'd take the kid and go to Australia. I'd love to go. The kid has a pet name—he's called Buck—and he loves bread and jam and I think he prefers me to her. I have to go now as she's calling me. Not a word to my mother about any of this. I'll let you know developments.

Your fond friend
Mary

PS. I am thinking of changing my name. How do you like the sound of Myrtle?

JOYCE CAROL OATES

Conquistador

And now here. Look. Friday, January 21, 6:15 pm. The dim, pinkly lit Costa del Sol lounge just off the main entrance of the Conquistador Motor Inn in Bethel Park, a suburb 20 miles north of Woodland. A solitary woman at the bar, in a high-necked but backless dress. A blonde woman. Attractive. Smoking a cigarette thoughtfully. Not frowning, not melancholy or troubled, but thoughtful. Mysterious. A woman of substance. Character. Sitting at the nearly deserted bar, pert and straight-backed and somehow provocative on one of the little leather stools, her waist and hips clearly defined in the clinging black silk dress, her naked back defiantly white: a woman Edwin Locke has never set eyes on before, smoking a cigarette languidly and stirring the ice in her drink.

Look. It is happening as he has planned. As he has rehearsed.

He enters the lounge hesitantly, almost timidly, though he knows that his appearance, this evening, is impressive (a new sports jacket, brown with brass buttons, and new dark trousers; his most attractive necktie, a beige knit; his hair freshly cut, shampooed and blown dry). A few of the patrons glance around, the bartender gives him an indifferent appraisal, but the woman does not seem to notice.

Edwin wonders. Is she alone at the Motor Inn? Or is she simply awaiting a husband or an escort? Or a lover? Sitting at the bar, waiting for a man. Her lover, perhaps. A woman like that *would* have a lover. Lovers.

He sees with a small thrill of excitement that her left hand is ringless. (She is wearing an oversized dinner ring on her right hand, possibly a topaz. Is it in bad taste, or is it merely daring, a flamboyant gesture? It seems clear from the way she plays with the swizzle stick in her drink that she is an independent, perhaps even a somewhat spoiled woman.) Unmarried. Solitary. Very attractive—very. And so, timidly, and boldly, Edwin Locke approaches the bar. His silly heart is pounding. Veins at his temples are pounding.

The risk of it. Once again. The blind gasping plunge.

Cheerfully he has said to himself, up in the room, dabbing cologne on his throat, his jaw: What can I lose? What can I lose?

Ah, the woman *is* attractive. Heavily but skilfully made up. Sharply defined lips, very red. Stylish hair, wavy, shaved up the back of her slender neck. Tiny gold earrings for pierced ears. A somewhat snubbed nose. And that bare, palely gleaming back, the tiny knuckle-bones of vertebrae, a sight that Edwin finds mesmerizing, as if he has never seen anything like it before.

'Are you ... May I join ...'

He swallows his words miserably. So timid! Such a fool! The woman finally looks around, her lips parting damply, in expectation. Her carefully arched eyebrows register a cool, almost contemptuous curiosity. Edwin repeats his question, smiling like an adolescent boy, and the woman stares at him in silence. Her eyes are thickly outlined with black pencil, brightly keen. She is young. Well, fairly. A mature woman with a glowing, youthful, sensuous face. It is obvious from the way she sits at the bar, her breasts pressing against the leather rim, that she is a sensuous, experienced woman, a woman of mysterious substance and character. It is obvious that ...

Edwin pulls a bar stool over. Sits. Sweating, smiling. He orders a scotch from the bored bartender, who is dressed in a toreador jacket. He asks the woman if she is alone. Or waiting for someone. Alone? Yes. Alone. Asks her what she is drinking. And would

she like another. Yes? The lounge is quite attractive, isn't it. The
black leather, the red and pink lampshades. The bull-fighting
motif in a bronze bas-relief above the bar. The Conquistador
itself is quite attractive, one of the newer motels in this area. The
restaurant, they say, is quite adequate. Over-priced (aren't they
all) but adequate.

The woman nods but her manner is still somewhat haughty,
withdrawn. Edwin tries to think of something to say, to ask. He
could inquire about her background: is she married, has she ever
been married, has she any children, has she been, well, *wounded* by
life, as he has? But she is so coolly remote, so tantalizingly
distant. Ah, she knows him—she knows how to tease! He hears
himself saying something about the weather. Ever since early
December it's been so grim and cheerless, hasn't it. And that
blizzard on New Year's Day. Funny, as you get older time is
supposed to go more rapidly, and in many ways it *does* (now why
in Christ's name am I saying this, Edwin wonders in dismay, but
cannot stop, and cannot change the subject), but that isn't true
of the weather, is it. In fact the winter seems to hang on forever.

'Yes. I suppose so,' the woman says neutrally.

What to say? He tries to remember what he has rehearsed. In
his imagination the woman was far more acquiescent, her face
was turned fully towards him, her lips and eyes melting . . . He
fumbles in his pocket for cigarettes. But with an exquisitely casual
gesture the woman pushes *her* pack towards him.

'Hey. Thanks. That's very sweet,' he whispers.

The woman's smile is wry and knowing. She is not young, nor
is she pretty any longer, despite her clever make-up; but Edwin
feels almost faint with excitement and apprehension. He leans
towards her, smiling. He inhales her perfume with gratitude.
Something musky, something very provocative. And the look of
her naked back, the tiny bones appearing to shiver slightly
beneath the fine, pale envelope of skin.

'You're very . . . You're . . .' He swallows suddenly. Has to
fight an impulse to cough, 'a very attractive woman. *Very* attractive.'

Her nostrils widen as she draws in her breath, considering his remark. Then she says with admirable evenness: '*You're* a very attractive man.'

Edwin sips his drink. Says quickly: 'As soon as I came in the doorway I noticed you. And wanted you. I mean that—just the way it sounds. I saw you sitting here and I wanted you, just like that. I'm the kind of man who . . . who . . . I'm the kind of man who knows what he likes, in a woman. Who is able to appreciate . . . who is able to appreciate a womanly woman. A woman who knows . . . who knows about certain things. Who isn't coy. Who isn't self-conscious. As soon as I saw you here I *knew*.'

The woman laughs lightly, but Edwin can see that he has startled her. 'Is that so,' she drawls.

'I imagine you know what you want too. In a man. I imagine you aren't shy about . . . about expressing yourself,' Edwin says softly.

Half-closes his eyes. Waits. What will happen next, what *should* happen next? He is quite excited. The woman is too, or should be. Sexual tension: unmistakable. The way she is sitting . . . the way she avoids his eye. She *should* be excited. Is. Is excited. Must try to imagine the sensations arising in her, in the pit of her belly, between her thighs, would it be an ache, would it be a nervous tingling feeling, a sense of . . . of yearning . . .? Yearning to be filled? Completed? By him? By *him*?

He lights a cigarette. Bloody damn nuisance: has to flick the lighter several times before a flame catches. One two three four *five*.

She lifts her glass. Drains it in one long swallow.

'A woman like you, with a . . . a body like yours . . . a mature, sensuous, *knowing* . . .'

'Mature?'

'Experienced. Widely and, and variedly . . . and knowledgeably experienced.'

The woman considers his words, staring at the glass in her hand. Edwin sees that her fingernails have been painted a

dramatic golden-bronze. How odd, how beguiling a colour! He
doesn't think he has ever seen it before, close up, on a real
woman, a *real* person. 'And you,' she whispers, 'what about you?'

'Me? Oh. Well. *Me*,' Edwin says, going blank for a moment. 'I
am . . . I am the kind of man . . . I am the kind of man, honey,
who knows what he likes. I mean I can appreciate . . . I can *see* . . .
Well, there are things that another man might not notice, but . . .
I have had some interesting experiences with women. Some very,
very interesting experiences.'

'Have you,' she says, a trifle sharply. And then, in a more
subdued throaty voice: 'Oh. *Have* you.'

'And the one thing I learned, the one thing I absolutely learned,
was . . . the one thing I am in fact *still* learning . . . is that a
woman's sensuality is far deeper and more complex and . . . and
astonishing . . . and even alarming . . . than a man's. This is
something all men should—'

'Alarming, why? Did you say alarming?'

'Astonishing. Amazing. Just fantastic,' Edwin says, shaking
his head. 'I mean *fantastic*. *You* know what I mean.'

The woman giggles suddenly. 'I'm not sure if I do.'

'Yes, you do. *You* know.'

'Do I?'

'With a, a body like yours . . . Those hips and . . . and breasts
. . . Your mouth . . . oh you know, you know,' he says, giggling
himself, trying hard to resist a sudden spasm of coughing. 'I
mean it stands out. It announces itself. Why, as soon as I came in
the door, the doorway, as soon as my gaze fastened on . . . Well
I mean I knew. I just knew. And,' he says lowering his voice,
trembling, 'I wanted you. In that instant.'

'Did you. Did you really,' the woman says.

'Obviously. Can't you tell.'

'Another drink?'

'Yes. Certainly. What time is it?'

'Early.'

'Early . . . Fine. Another drink. Two more, in fact. And then, do you think we might, do you think you'd enjoy ... well, coming upstairs with me?'

'To your room?'

'To my room. Where we can continue our discussion in privacy.'

'But we hardly know each other. I don't even know your name.'

'Is that important? Are names so important to you?'

She smirks. No, it is a smile, a frightened little smile.

'No. Of course not. You should be able to tell that, just by looking at me,' she says slowly, vaguely.

'The room is a very attractive one. In fact it's a honeymoon suite, I believe ... At a special discount.'

'What sort of discount?'

'A sunken bathtub, of marble, an enormous heart-shaped bed, a dozen pillows, a thick plush rug, lamps with shades of pink and scarlet, flowers, fresh flowers, and candles and incense. And on closed-circuit television, if we should want it, certain films, certain frankly *erotic* films ... as the advertising brochure says. But I don't really think, do you, that we will need such things,' Edwin says breathlessly.

'Is there music? There must be music,' the woman says, blushing faintly.

'I think so. Yes. Piped-in. Throbbing and sensual. Spanish, I think. Spanish flamenco. I think.'

'But we don't know each other. We don't know each other's *name.*'

Edwin laughs, raising his glass in a toast. His laughter becomes wheezing but he manages to get it under control. 'Name? Why? Such an out-moded convention ... And you don't look at all like a conventional woman.'

'Maybe I'm not. But still.'

'Beneath your clothes, for instance.'

'Beneath what? Why?'

'In your flesh. In your skin. *There* you aren't a conventional woman, are you? But all women. Sharing in their secrets ...'

She giggles suddenly. Finishes her drink. 'And now,' Edwin
says. 'Now. I think it's about time, don't you?'

'Well—'

'I *think* it's about time we adjourned to room 225.'

'Do you have the key?'

'Of course,' Edwin says, patting his pocket. The key is attached
to an oversized Spanish coin of plastic; he slipped it into his
pocket on the way down. But though his fingers fully expect to
touch the key they come away baffled. 'That is I think . . .'

The woman snatches up her purse. Opens it. Takes out a com-
pact. Dabs at her nose with a powder puff, rather impatiently.
'Have you lost the key?' she asks.

'It's here somewhere. It must be,' Edwin mutters. He searches
the pockets of his sports coat. Odd. Very odd. He tries his
trouser pockets. No? But where? *Is* it lost? Did someone pick
his pocket on the way down? Or? 'Oh Christ,' he says, 'I put it
in my other coat. I was going to wear my other coat . . . Not that
it matters. of course. I can pick another key up at the front desk.'

The woman closes her purse with an angry snap. Edwin sees,
surprised, that her expression is stiff with bemused contempt.
'Can you?' she whispers. 'Can you really?'

'What do you mean? I don't . . . I don't understand . . .'

'Tonight of all nights. Deliberately. And you're drunk, aren't
you. You were drinking before you met me. And you saw to it
that I'm drunk. Didn't you. And that tie—the dry cleaner never
got that gravy stain out of it, can't you see? Can't you for God's
sake *see*? I thought I'd thrown that thing out years ago but somehow you still *have* it, you must have *hoarded* it . . .' She begins to
cry, her shoulders shaking, her face distorted. 'Tonight of all
nights. Oh Edwin, *tonight of all nights.*'

'But . . . but . . . But I can pick up another key at the front desk,
can't I?' Edwin asks, astonished.

CARYL BRAHMS

A Bishop in the Ballet

Evening in Santa Fé, with the distant snow mountains rose-
tipped in the sunset and the Ballet Stroganov guesting at the
Opera House. It was the off-season.

Vladimir Stroganov was sitting in the Presidential Box, a carnation resplendent in his buttonhole, his bald dome shining with
enthusiasm, beaming at the spectacle his company was presenting.
Beside him sat the Bishop of Chi-hua-hua, an unlikely companion,
all things considered.

On-stage a gaggle of swans were doing their somewhat bleary
best.

In the Stage Box, Madame Arenskaya, the Ballet Stroganov's
spirited Maitresse-de-Ballet, was being restrained with difficulty
from hurling a shoe at the simpering Prince, currently a young—
well, middle-aged—Master Eyelashes with a receding hairline,
who had bought himself into the Stroganov company and bribed
his way into a few leading roles though he was in no way ready
for the honour, in Madame Arenskaya's frequently expressed
opinion.

Stroganov glowed at the Bishop: 'My company is perfection,
no?'

'No,' said the Bishop, deciding for once not to hide the truth
under a biretta.

Fortunately the headlong Stroganov had not stopped talking to
listen to him. 'Wait only till you see our *Giselle*—the mad scene,'

he specified, and ticked it off on one podgy finger, 'our *Boutique Fantasque,*' he continued ticking off should-be masterpieces, 'our *Oiseau de Feu,*' he ticked, 'our *Sylphides* ' he ticked, 'our . . . our . . .' he sought for a ballet to clinch his argument, 'our *No Holds Barred,* a Nevajno work, *bien moderne*; the scene it is a boxing ring, in,' he paused for dramatic effect, 'Outer Space.'

'You have run out of fingers,' observed the Bishop, coldly.

'Me,' announced Stroganov, 'I envy you who are seeing the fabled Ballet Stroganov for the first time. What rapture awaits you!'

'This a rapture?' The Bishop of Chi-hua-hua did not sound convinced. He gazed disbelieving at the middle-aged young Master Eyelashes who at that moment was surrounded by, but alas! not lost in, a group of depressed swans.

'That one,' said Stroganov dispassionately, 'is a geese. But he is rich, so each time Arenskaya give him sack, he give me bribe,' he rubbed his hands, 'so me I take him back.'

In the Stage Box Arenskaya was turning to her companion, an antique General who had attached himself to the company, in what capacity no-one could say.

'Heneral,' she ordered, 'oblige me, *mon cher*, go to my dressing-room and bring me my pearls I have borrowed—Sheherazade,' she explained all—'without my pearls I am non-stop Nude.'

'Aie!' said the General alarmed and creaked away.

Freed from his restraining presence Arenskaya removed a shoe in readiness.

The curtain fell but rose again immediately lest the audience should take it seriously. The ballet itself was at an end. So now the real business of the evening began. The bows and the bouquets. First the Corps-de-Ballet scampered on with not an hibiscus among them. Then four soloists lined up and advanced to what the great Fokine designated 'The Tootsies.' Each soloiste clasping to her non-existent bosom the flowers sent by Mamoushka, husband, or self. From the crimson and gold splendours of the Presidential Box, Stroganov applauded vigorously. 'You do not clap for my children?' he asked the Bishop incredulously.

The Bishop, recalled from whatever holy theme he had been pondering, clapped obediently; but Stroganov could tell that the Episcopal heart was not in it. And he was right. The Bishop had been thinking how to get a receptacle full of white heroin tablets through the inquisitive British Customs. He was no common or garden Bishop. He was a common or garden Pusher.

Now it was the turn of the Swan Princess—gin would not melt in her mouth, but a great many carbohydrates had. She stepped forward clasping her flowers to her stomach of which, currently, there was no lack. The Bishop answered to his cue and clapped loudly. Stroganov grabbed the holy hands.

'Me, I do not applaud this one,' he protested. 'She has the Mamoushka money-conscious! Already now she has eye on Presidential Box—this Box,' he could not resist boasting. 'So me, I sit on the hands,' he demonstrated.

By now it was the turn of the middle-aged young Master Eye-lashes with the receding hairline to bound on boyishly. He bowed to the Presidential Box, he bowed to the audience, he bounded off into the wings. 'That one,' said Stroganov admiringly, 'is a bounder. The pity is, he does not dance so good, Arenskaya is right; but do not tell her so for it is bad for her character.'

'Ah!' said the Bishop. He placed his fingertips together and surveyed the stage, gazing over the tops of his rimless spectacles, as the bounder bounded back on-stage. Once again, he bowed to the Gallery, to the Family Circle, to the Grand Tier, to the stalls and finally, a grave mistake, to the Stage Box.

'Now,' breathed Madame Arenskaya. She hurled.

The brou-ha! ha! had all but subsided. Vladimir Stroganov mopping his brow, bobbed up from behind the Bishop, where he had been hiding from the wrath, which, born optimist that he was, he hoped was not to come.

'Quick, little Father,' he implored, 'we make the getaway

damnquick and lock ourselves in my office before they start the
cry and hue. The tequila and soda awaits us there: we have the
little sozzle before the rich one with the eyelashes comes to demand his bribes back. And later, when all is over and the little
Mothers are marching their little daughters straight back to their
little hotels, for the morals in my company are very strict, you
understand, we risk back-stage together.' The Bishop blinked.
'We take the Rich one with the eyelashes and the tide-out hairline
to supper to console him. Arenskaya we do not take; always she
demand the gipsy music and always it end in tears.'

'But,' said the Bishop . . . he fumbled for his indigestion capsules.

'You go pale, little Father, but the Rich one will pay. I offer him
another spectacular rôle so he pays now and later I take the rôle
away and he give me spectacular bribe to get it back again. There
are,' said Stroganov happily, 'always ways.'

'Ho-hum!' said the Bishop.

'But for now it is the tip-toe through the tulips—you get me?'

The Bishop did. The tip-toe was mother's milk to a Pusher.
Together the ill-assorted couple crept out. The corridor gained,
a shrill voice brought them to a halt. It was Arenskaya, one shoe
on—the other was in the incensed grasp of the Eyelash one in
hysterics in his dressing room. 'Vladimir,' she shrilled, 'you go
at once to the dressing-room of the Eyelash one and you demand
back my shoe I have borrowed from Dyrakova who is away and
do not know she lend—she dance *La Folle de Chaillot*, *chez* the
Beryl Grey, a long woman. But she come back to us tomorrow.'

'*La Folle de Chaillot* will not have the look-in when Dyrakova
find out you have borrow again,' opined Stroganov; 'when
Dyrakova go mad she have a *grandeur* unmatchable.'

'Me, I am no joke at the going mad,' Arenskaya boasted to the
unintroduced Bishop. 'Tiens! I like your shirt—purple suit you.'
She turned her back on Stroganov. 'Alors?' she urged. She placed
her hands on her hips (Zizi Jeanmaire—in *Carmen*). She tossed
her bright red head. She waited. Stroganov read the signs.

'Why throw, my darlink?' he pointed to the slipper. 'Why you not think first?'

'But this I do,' said the aggrieved Arenskaya, 'I think there is the dancer world-wide-worst. I think I throw Dyrakova's shoe at him, and then, mon cher, I throw.' She turned for sympathy to the Bishop. She jerked her crimson curls in the direction of the Pass Door. 'Go Vladimir, go at once—at once—or else . . .' She propped herself against the Bishop to take off Dyrakova's other shoe. She shook it at Stroganov. 'Or else . . .'

'Do not impatient yourself, my darlink. We go at once, my new chum and me. Hand in foot we go together.'

'Ah bon!' Arenskaya said. She relaxed.

Up in his office Stroganov was his own man again. He motioned the Bishop to the armchair. He poured tequila with a lavish hand. He himself sat on the revolving chair behind the desk. He spun round on it—sheer swank—and when he had come to rest the pair of them toasted each other. 'Should auld acquaintance be forgot,' intoned the Bishop.

'This they will never let you do,' Stroganov shook a realistic head: 'Or they are after you for the free seat, or they are after you for the money you owe them.'

'Then,' the Bishop suggested, 'we will drink to new friends.'

'New friends,' said Stroganov enthusiastically. They drank.

'There is a little matter I would like to discuss,' the Bishop looked around him furtively—for a Bishop, that is.

'You can confide in me,' said Stroganov. 'My office it is sacrosanct. No one comes here and if they do I kick them out damn-quick.'

'Ho-hum!' said the Bishop. He polished his rimless spectacles.

Should any reader ask himself how Stroganov and the Bishop became 'the chums bosom' the answer is easy.

Both had been gazing wistfully at the windows of the local Tiffany's. Stroganov was attracted immediately by the bright shade of pink that passes for purple in a Bishop. Remember that it is out of season at Santa Fé. Barons and Bishops are hard to come by. If only he could capture this one and seat him beside himself, in the Presidential Box it would dress his house which badly needed it. As to the Pusher, he was looking for a credulous individual to carry his heroin through the Customs for him. Stroganov fitted the bill. Was not his despatch case much labelled with the names of far-away lands?

The next two hours the enstomached gentlemen wasted cautiously stalking one another. Finally thirst put an end to caution, and they found themselves sitting side by side at a little table outside the Taverna in the Plaza.

For a time they conversed amiably—The cost of living. The cost of lemon-tea. The cost of politicians. The cost. Then Stroganov popped the question—'You come to my box at the Ballet to-night? I give you card.' He scribbled.

The Pusher whistled a happy tune. The Mexican heroin was as good as in the Chelsea bag.

Back at the office the Bishop was putting his head as close to Stroganov's bald dome as the latter's revolving chair permitted. Next to his ballet, his revolving chair was the pride of Stroganov's life. He travelled it everywhere with him.

'My friend,' the Bishop was intoning, 'I have not known you long as time goes, but there is something about you that inspires confidence.'

'My chair?' Stroganov gave it a twirl. 'In me,' he announced when it came to rest, 'you can have the confidence absolute.'

'You see,' the Bishop lowered his voice, 'it is—ah!—a family affair, and in my position . . .'

'I am the soul of discretion,' announced Stroganov.

'I do not even tell the Eyelash one with the money to make the

mouth water in the letter from his wife with the oil-well in Texas—
which remind me,' he leaped up from his seat and studied the
calendar on the wall. 'This month she is late already. But no
matter; he has much jewellery she give him. With this he can
raise the Hurricane.' The Bishop blinked. 'And so, little Father,
you can count on the secrecy absolute. We are cosy here, no?
No one dare to come to my sanctum to disturb me.' Stroggy
twirled.

'Sit still like a good chap,' said the Bishop, 'and listen atten-
tively. Back home in Chelsea, England, I have an aged grandmother,' the Bishop confided.

'No kidding?' asked Stroganov, looking pointedly at his white
locks.

'See this wet, see this dry?' said the forgetful Pusher. He
blushed.

'And this aged one, she is in the trouble financial?' asked
Stroganov from out of a wealth of experience.

'The trouble physical,' said the Pusher. Stroganov's misplaced
English was getting to him. 'If my old grandmother does not
get her fix—I mean the medicament I shall give you for her . . .'

'She gerfut?'

'She gerfut,' agreed the Bishop.

'Then why you not take it to her damnquick?' Stroganov
demanded, reasonably enough.

'I have duties—Ecclesiastical duties—to perform in Mexico,'
his new friend explained. 'Perhaps you would be a . . .' the Pusher
bethought himself. From out of his small store of Bible stories
learnt at the Borstal Chaplain's knee, he produced ' "Good
Samaritan" and take this package to Chelsea. And there a—mm—
colleague of mine will relieve you of your trust and convey it to
my ancient grandmother.'

'*Bien sûr*,' Stroganov beamed. 'Before everything me I am the
Samaritan good—for the moment,' he added with unusual
caution.

The Bishop had recourse to his indigestion tablet. 'You come to my box—the Presidential box,' urged Stroganov, 'tomorrow night and you give me your little grandmother's medicaments.'

'And you do not tell a living soul?'

'Not a syllable to a sturgeon,' swore Stroganov. He took off in his revolving chair.

The door burst open. It was Arenskaya.

'Sit still, Vladimir,' she commanded.

Stroganov frowned. 'What you do in my sanctum, old chum?'

'I . . . I . . . I . . .' Arenskaya stuttered. She reared her head like a good Russian goose.

'You . . . you . . . you . . .' greatly daring Stroganov mimicked her. 'In future, you knock. Then I call out go away and you vamoose damnquick. You must understand I am busy here with my new chum and the matter confidential about his ancient grandmother.'

'Ho-hum!' The Bishop cast a warning look at Stroganov. But on that one it was lost for already he was in full if broken spate.

'The little Father entrust me with the medicaments for his ancient grandmamoushka, and I have give my word—the word of a Stroganov, woman—not to tell a living creature, and not you, it is certain, that I take the packet to England and give it to . . . and give it to . . . to whom do I give it?' he enquired of the sweating Bishop, who was quite bereft of words.

There was a sharp knock at the door. 'Go away,' called Stroganov. He twirled. Relentlessly the door opened and in came an irate Mamoushka trailing her hesitant daughter, that night's Swan Princess.

'Sit still, Stroganov,' she said. 'We have come to plead our stomach.' She pointed to her daughter's protruding abdomen and patted her own for emphasis. 'We are *enceinte*,' she added, unnecessarily.

Arenskaya took in the stomach at a glance. 'She is right, Vladimir,' she concurred, 'she is *enceinte*, and this is why she keep leaving my *Classe de Perfection* and lock herself in the loo, where she brings up.'

'We need money,' said Mamoushka.

'The advance generous,' suggested Arenskaya, evilly playing Stroganov out for some ancient injury—she had forgotten which.

'On whose side you are?' he asked hotly. Then at bay, he turned on Mamoushka and daughter. 'You go away. It is out of hours, and me, I am busy with the Bishop. I have to write myself a note to remind me what to do with the medicament for the little grandmother. It is the errand of mercy, you understand, and also the matter confidential, so me I don't tell no-one.' He looked at the apoplectic Pusher. He winked.

There was a knock at the door. It was the middle-aged young Master Eyelashes. But the assembled company could not know this.

'Stay out!' they called as one man. 'Go away,' they added. 'And don't come back no more,' screeched Arenskaya solo.

The Eyelash one blinked. He decided to bivouac outside Stroganov's office, if necessary for the night. 'We Eyelashes,' he reminded himself, 'We Eyelashes hang on by ourselves.'

For the next week the little grandmother of the Bishop was the name on the lips of everyone remotely concerned with the Stroganov Company and even some quite unconnected with it. But it was not until after the Bishop called at the Box Office to collect the pass to Stroganov's box ('The Presidential Box,' pointed out the Box Office Manager, bowing with touching respect. 'And how, my Lord, is the health of the Little Grandmother these days?') that he remonstrated with Stroganov again.

Up in his office Stroganov was in full spate. 'But I tell you,' he was shouting into the telephone, 'I pay the creditors all, all, all— but not my tailor. The ancient little grandmum of my new chum, the Bishop, has for me the gratitude immense, or will have, when I give the fellow in Chelsea the capsules which keep her ticking.'

'Vladimir,' said the Bishop, shocked, for the friendship had flowered into Christian names. 'You gave me your word that you would not tell a soul.'

Stroganov nodded violently, 'It is the matter undisclosable,' he told the telephone. 'My lips are sealed and you must say nothing to no-one, and specially not to my tailor—*entendu*? *Eh bien, mon cher Esteban, au revoir.*' He put down the phone. He gave his chair a twirl. 'And now, old chum,' he said, 'what is new?'

'You promised, Vladimir. You promised you would not disclose a syllable.'

'To a sturgeon. This, Francesco, I remember. And I have only told a fat little pigeon in the second row, who is my new love personal, and—and the Master Eyelash one, instead of the rise he covet; and still the wife in Texas does not send the money needed urgent.

'And the Manager Bank, him I tell for sure, and the Company Physiotherapist,—that one he pommel it out of me!'

The phone rang. Stroganov applied himself to it and in a babble of Bishops, new chums, Grandmamoushkas, capsules and gerfuts told the disembodied enquirer all—or as near all as made no difference.

The Bishop looked at the ceiling. It remained oblivious.

'But who were you telling on the telephone, Vladimir?'

'Poof!' Stroganov dismissed the disembodied voice, 'That one was my very old friend from the British Customs, so we have nothing to fear.'

The Bishop seemed to be having breathing trouble. But Stroganov appeared not to notice this. From his desk he picked up a bill. It was one of many. He glared at it. 'My tailor,' he observed, 'is the disgust. He demand small fortune and besides his suit it did not fit, for the food in the Americas South it is very rich with oil and olives, and me, I like good blow-out very much and . . . and . . . well see for yourself, Francesco—the suit across the estomach do not meet.'

He breathed out. A button popped.

Sir Arbuthnot Chiddingfold, continent to continent, as he boasted to the disinterested operator:

''Allo . . . 'allo . . . 'Allo- 'Allo- 'Allo!' Stroganov was jiggling the instrument so no croak from the other end could thread its way to him. 'Is that you, *mon cher*? I wish you to write to the manager of my London bank in Cheapside—cheap, I ask you?— to say if he do not stop pursuing me with his boring demands I will cancel my overdraft. And to my tailor that I cannot be bothered with his silly bills and . . . and . . . to the little grandmother of the Bishop of Chi-hua-hua . . .'

At this point Sir Arbuthnot slammed down the receiver, causing Stroganov to erupt into a storm of 'Allo, 'Allos and jiggering at the end of which he took a refreshing twirl in his chair. The enemies had been silenced, or soon would be. All was mooch better in the best of all possible worlds.

A glazed look passed over the Bishop's eyes. It was just such a look that might be found in a cod's eye on the fishmonger's cold marble slab. Should he kill off his little grandmamoushka forthwith and scotch the danger that surely must be lurking in the future! and yet . . . the Pusher thought of the money there was in the capsules. The Bishop thought of the Santa Féan jail. Beneath the petunia robe they were sporting both Bishop and Pusher engaged in a man-to-man struggle. Greed won the day.

And what of the middle-aged young Master Eyelashes? Well, actually he was on the Balleto-osteopath's couch. The Balleto-osteopath, no mean judge of Ballet, was pommelling.

'That's for your Prince Igor . . .'

'Ouch!'

'And that's for your Florizel.'

'Ouch!'

'And *this* is for *Sylphides*.'

'Ouch!'

The Balleto-osteopath executed an involved and particularly painful joint-shaker.

'And this?' asked the Victim, 'it is for *Giselle*, no doubt?'

'No doubt at all,' said the Balleto-osteopath. He went on pommelling.

That night the Company seemed inspired—at least to Stroganov.
'They'ave dedicated this performance to the little Grandmum,'
he explained to the dozing Bishop.

From swan to swan, gosling to gosling, soloist to soloist, and
even the semi-dormant Benno, the Prince's friend, the word was
whispered. 'The tablets for the antique grandmamoushka. How
happy she will be when she has them safe in her hands. Nothing
shall befall them, we have sworn,' vowed the swans, 'to the last
Drake.'

There was a thud. The semi-dormant Benno had failed to catch
the night's ballerina, a Yugoslavian dancer. She picked herself up
from the stage. She could be seen to be swearing good round
Armenian oaths.

The Ballet went on.

Time passed. Nothing out of the ordinary at Heathrow Airport,
that afternoon. Just the usual mix of overheated travellers,
Japanese, American, Indian, Blacks and the po' white British,
plus a racing-round of everyone's kids. No, nothing out of the
ordinary.

Yet what was this bald-headed old buffer at the Customs Bench
using his arms like a protesting windmill, trying to snatch back a
tin from the Customs Officer who had opened it. 'But it is the
medicaments for the Bishop's Grandmamoushka, like I say,'
Stroganov was shouting. 'This is so,' said his whole company
and one elderly Russian General, grouped round him.

'Without her medicaments she gerfut,' Stroganov persisted.

'She gerfut,' agreed his indignant company.

'So you oblige us, and tell no-one,' Stroganov urged, 'for the
Bishop he not forgive you if it transpires.'

But the Customs were adamant.

'Non! Non! I tell you Non! I do not smuggle for the money.
I have no need. Or shall have when the pocket-money for the
Eyelash one shall arrive from the rich wife in Dallas.'

'Nonetheless,' said the Customs—they could be adamantine, too.

Somewhere unbeknown to Stroganov sweating in the held-up and cursing about it queue, a Bishop was feeling very, very sick. He fumbled for his tin of indigestion tablets. He swallowed one. It had the most extraordinary effect. He could have sworn that he was floating.

Three hours had passed. 'But you do not understand,' Stroganov was shouting to the plainclothes Detective at Bow Street Police Station, 'first I demand my Man-of-law. He is for the moment in New York, so you get on the telephone damnquick.'

'But,' said Inspector Lawless, paling, 'New York—that's in America.'

'*Précisément*,' Stroganov agreed. 'We will speak Continent to Continent—at expense of police.' He pounced. He jiggled. ''Allo, 'Allo, 'Allo, 'Allo,' he began expectantly.

But this time Detective Lawless, too, pounced and attempted to snatch. 'Oh no you don't.' The Detective tugged. Stroganov held on. Deadlock.

Suddenly Stroganov bethought him of another ploy, and let go. 'Get me Inspective Detector Quill,' he commanded.

Detective Inspector Lawless blanched again. 'Quill? Adam Quill?'

'Damnquick,' said Stroganov purposefully.

Detective Lawless mopped his brow. Clearly he was out of his depth. 'But Mr Quill—I mean, he's the Assistant Commissioner.'

'Ah, bon,' Stroganov beamed. 'Then he assist me, you will see.'

At that moment a Presence made itself felt. Commissioner Quill, suitably be-buttoned, and tailor-made, had emerged from some glorious inner office to see what the brouhaha outside was about.

Overjoyed, Stroganov threw his arms around him and kissed him on both cheeks.

Inspector Lawless could scarcely believe the evidence of his eyes.

'Monsieur Quill,' cried Stroganov, 'My old chum Inspective detector!' He hugged the aggrandized but unresisting Quill. 'You tell this policeman it is all the fault of the little grandmum of The Bishop one.'

'You heard, Lawless,' the Assistant Commissioner barked. 'Release Stroggy—Mister Stroganov.'

'Damnquick,' said Stroganov.

'Exactly,' said Commissioner Quill.

'And we go at once to your office and have the whisky-and-soda, and the smoke-salmon sandwiches appetising, while I tell you about the antique grandmamoushka, the Bishop, and the capsules entrusted to me. Without them our grandmamoushka she gerfut.'

'This way,' said the Assistant Commissioner weakly.

And that is how certain clients in Chelsea paid an all-time high for bicarbonate of soda.